PENGUIN BOOKS

BEYOND THE BLUE MOUNTAINS

Penelope Lively grew up in Egypt but settled in England after the war and took a degree in history at St Anne's College, Oxford. She is a Fellow of the Royal Society of Literature, and a member of PEN and the Society of Authors. She is married to Professor Jack Lively, has a daughter, a son and four grandchildren, and lives in Oxfordshire and London.

Penelope Lively is the author of many prize-winning novels and short story collections for both adults and children. She has twice been shortlisted for the Booker Prize: once in 1977 for her first novel, *The Road to Lichfield*, and again in 1984 for *According to Mark*. She later won the 1987 Booker Prize for her highly acclaimed novel *Moon Tiger*. Her novels include *Passing On*, shortlisted for the 1989 *Sunday Express* Book of the Year Award, *City of the Mind*, *Cleopatra's Sister* and *Heat Wave*. Many of her books, including *Going Back*, which first appeared as a children's book, and *Oleander, Jacaranda*, an autobiographical memoir of her childhood days in Egypt, are published in Penguin.

Penelope Lively has also written radio and television scripts and has acted as presenter for a BBC Radio 4 programme on children's literature. She is a popular writer for children and has won both the Carnegie Medal and the Whitbread Award.

D0816007

TITLES BY PENELOPE LIVELY IN PENGUIN

Fiction

Going Back
The Road to Lichfield
Treasures of Time
Judgement Day
Next to Nature, Art
Perfect Happiness
According to Mark
Pack of Cards: Collected Short Stories 1978–1986
Moon Tiger
Passing On
City of the Mind
Cleopatra's Sister
Heat Wave
Beyond the Blue Mountains

Autobiography

Oleander, Jacaranda: A Childhood Perceived

PENELOPE LIVELY

Beyond the Blue Mountains

PENGUIN BOOKS

PENGUIN BOOKS

Published by the Penguin Group
Penguin Books Ltd, 27 Wrights Lane, London W8 5TZ, England
Penguin Putnam Inc., 375 Hudson Street, New York, New York 10014, USA
Penguin Books Australia Ltd, Ringwood, Victoria, Australia
Penguin Books Canada Ltd, 10 Alcorn Avenue, Toronto, Ontario, Canada M4V 3B2
Penguin Books (NZ) Ltd, 182–190 Wairau Road, Auckland 10, New Zealand

Penguin Books Ltd, Registered Offices: Harmondsworth, Middlesex, England

This collection first published by Viking 1997
Published in Penguin Books 1998
1 3 5 7 9 10 8 6 4 2

'Beyond the Blue Mountains' was previously published in *The Traveller* and *Telling Stories, Vol. 2*
(Hodder & Stoughton); 'The Children of Grupp' in *Prize Writing* (Hodder & Stoughton); 'In
Olden Times' in *Good Housekeeping*; 'Season of Goodwill' in the *Illustrated London News*; 'The
Clarinettist and the Bride's Aunt', 'A Christmas Card to One and All', 'The First Wife' and
'Loved Ones' in *Living*; 'Marriage Lines' and 'The Butterfly and the Tin of Paint' in the
Daily Telegraph; 'The Five Thousand and One Nights' in the *Observer* and in *Best Stories 1989*
(Heinemann); and 'Crumbs of Wisdom' in *New Woman*

The moral right of the author has been asserted

Printed in England by Clays Ltd, St Ives plc

Contents

Beyond the Blue Mountains

Myra and George Purbeck, aboard the Empress of Sydney, rode through the Hawkesbury River valley. The Empress of Sydney was a coach, of an extravagance that neither had ever before experienced, a double-decker with picture windows of tinted glass, luxuriantly upholstered seating and small tilted movie screens lest the voyager should weary of the landscape. From time to time a stewardess plied them with coffee or freshly squeezed orange juice. The air-conditioning was just right; the restful and uninsistent background music was interrupted periodically by a voice which delivered a laconic, informative and sometimes witty account of the passing scene. They had been given a run-down of the social composition of suburban Sydney, with a digression on architectural style. They had learned about the crops grown in the farmland through which they now passed and about breeds of cattle and of sheep. 'Look left and you'll see three black swans on a billabong. The black swan is native to Australia.' Myra listened with interest.

She said, 'Is it the driver who does this commentary, do you imagine?'

'Presumably.' George was reading – intermittently – a copy of the London *Financial Times*. He was also, of course, gathering strength for the next leg of an exacting business trip. It was Sunday. The coach trip was for Myra's benefit: a kindly indulgence.

In Sydney, while George performed business, she had wandered, at first jet-lagged and punch-drunk. She felt as though she had stepped into an alternative universe. The birds that flew in the garden of their hotel were little parrots, she saw with astonishment. The trees and shrubs were eerie and beautiful developments of familiar trees and shrubs. The very air seemed different. Then she had gone into an art gallery and seen on the walls a further miraculous transformation of the known world. The paintings showed a brilliant landscape, vibrant with colour – blues and golds and a bright ochre, a place of rock and dust and tree that was vast, bold and disturbing. Some of the pictures were of forest scenes – they depicted dappled light, sparkling water and exuberant growth. In one, an aborigine family camped around a fire in a clearing. Wallabies grazed, the trees were roped with flowering vines, shafts of light fell on emerald grass. Myra gazed in fascination; words she did not normally use flew into her head – a glade, an arcadian glade. Emerging once more into the heat and sunshine of the city, she was elated. The jet-lag faded. She began to feel unusually alert and well.

In the evenings they dined with business associates of George's, who asked her what she thought of Oz and then moved on to other matters without listening to her answer. George smiled benignly and sometimes he replied on her behalf, saying that Myra was having a fine old time in the shopping malls. He had brought her on this trip because she was on his conscience.

The coach began to climb. They had left the farmland behind and were entering the foothills of the Blue Mountains. The Blue Mountains, explained the invisible commentator, are thus named because of the sun's effect on the haze of oil vapour given off by eucalyptus trees. At the beginning of the nineteenth century they formed an impenetrable barrier between the expanding settlement and the hinterland beyond, until the pioneering expedition of Blaxland, Lawson and Wentworth in 1813, which led to the construction within six months of the first road through the mountains by hand-picked convict labourers.

Myra looked through the rose-tinted windows of the Empress of Sydney at the steep slopes, the rock, the soaring trees. The coach, now, swung around hairpin bends.

She said, 'Six months . . . It's incredible.'

George was busy with his laptop. He lifted his eyes and stared for a few moments out of the window. He became reflective. Myra doubted that his thoughts were on Blaxland, Lawson and Wentworth or, indeed, the convicts.

The coach was sparsely populated. Up here on the top deck there were six immaculately suited Japanese who sat together in a cluster, a couple of backpacking American girls and a waste of empty seats. The commentator began to talk of flora and fauna. He told the passengers to look for tree-ferns, for casuarinas and for sulphur-crested cockatoos. When they reached the viewpoint and the revolving restaurant they must take a stroll and listen for bellbirds. If anyone had any questions feel free to hand a note to the stewardess.

Myra tore a page out of her diary. She wrote, 'What are the scarlet flowers on low bushes?' She gave it to the stewardess.

Five minutes later, the coach drew up at the roadside. Myra, looking down through the window, saw a lanky figure drop from the driver's compartment and vanish into the undergrowth of the steep hillside. A minute later he reappeared, leapt back up into the coach. They moved off once more. 'In fifteen minutes or so we shall reach the famous viewpoint, where you have a two-hour stop to enjoy the wonderful views beyond the Blue Mountains. Take a ride across the valley on the funicular railway, have a walk in the bush but be careful to stick to the paths – easy to get lost in this country. And you'll get a fine three-course meal in the revolving restaurant. Have a good time. And for the passenger who's interested in flowers – it's red honey-flower. Mountain devil, we call it.'

The stewardess had arrived at Myra's elbow. She held out a tray on which was perched a spray of silky scarlet flowers. 'With the driver's compliments.'

Myra picked up the flowers. 'Thank you.' She tucked them into the top buttonhole of her shirt. She felt a surge of gaiety, a swoop of well-being which exactly matched the exuberance of the blossoms.

They arrived at their destination – a complex of cafés and restaurants at the highest point of the mountain range. The various viewpoints looked out across an apparently endless sequence of blue-green ridges splashed here and there with the rich brown of a rock face. Myra, alighting from the coach, was again seized with exhilaration. This place is doing something to me, she thought. It was as though she had shed a skin, and stepped out new-minted and charged with life.

There were the restaurants, and the ticket office for the funicular railway, which swooped dizzyingly down over the mountainside. And there all around them beyond the car park were stretches of dappled woodland that made her think at once of that painting. She saw tree-ferns, with grey scaly trunks and a brilliant eruption of bracken-like leaves. She saw the ropes of flowering creepers, the bright grass on which quivered gold coins of sunlight. She looked for grazing wallabies, and a tranquil aborigine family.

She said, 'Let's go for a walk.'

But George preferred to sit on the restaurant terrace with a beer. He had some phone calls to make, too. Ah yes, thought Myra, no doubt. 'Fine,' she said. 'I'll walk for a bit and come back for lunch. In this revolving restaurant, I suppose.'

She visited the toilets, and then set off. She chose a narrow path which looked the least frequented, and followed it into the trees. And instantly she heard a bellbird – a clear, sweet, chiming sound from some invisible presence high in the waving branches.

The trees thinned out. There was a clearing. And there in the clearing, leaned up against a rock reading a newspaper, with a sandwich in one hand and a can of Coke alongside, was a man. A long, rangy man in ubiquitous Aussie gear – shirt, shorts and knee socks. Myra prepared to walk tactfully past.

He looked up. 'Hi, there,' he said. 'Enjoying the trip?'

She put two and two together. Of course. The driver.

'I certainly am. And thank you for the flowers.'

'My pleasure.'

She had slowed up only very slightly. Now she was alongside him, and starting to move away.

'Take care,' he said. 'Stick to the path.'

'I will,' said Myra. 'And I heard a bellbird.'

'Great,' said the driver. He was looking directly at her and the look, she suddenly saw, was one of appreciation, genial and in no way offensive. I like what I see, it said. Maybe we could have got together, under other circumstances.

He raised his paper. She walked on.

Well, thought Myra. Well.

She was not a vain woman, never had been. She saw herself, objectively, as the sort of person who is not much noticed. Unassertive. This, perhaps, accounted for much.

And now, here, in this interesting other world, she felt different. And, it would seem, appeared differently.

The path looped round in a circle and returned her to the car park and to the restaurant terrace. She cruised in, walking tall, hungry, brisk and seeing everything very sharp and clear. Her husband, sitting there with his laptop, his newspaper and his beer.

They sat opposite one another in the revolving restaurant. Myra chose a seafood salad, avoiding the Filet of Buffalo with Confit of Beetroot. George ate a steak, medium rare.

They spoke, briefly, of arrangements for the following day, of a handbag Myra had purchased for her sister, of a difficulty George was experiencing with his computer. Myra told him of the bellbird. She spoke of other birds she had noticed – the rosellas in the hotel garden, a kookaburra on a gatepost by the roadside. As she talked she saw the mountain ranges inch slowly past George's head. They sat within a creeping sphere, a dramatic and sumptuous backcloth quite at odds with the clatter of knives and forks, the red-checked napery and the chomping diners. Myra's sense of disorientation became acute. Disorientation, and a certain wild confidence.

George was not listening to her. He was looking beyond her left shoulder. His eyes were blank. She knew what he was thinking about. He was thinking about Bridget Cashell, his mistress.

She said, 'You're thinking about Bridget Cashell, your mistress, aren't you?'

Mistress. She relished the word. It had overtones of satin

dressing-gowns. Bridget Cashell was in fact accounts manager in George's firm and, although distinctly personable, was not at all the satin dressing-gown type. Myra listened to her own words with astonishment and satisfaction.

George too listened, apparently. His eyes leapt to life. Myra saw surprise, dismay and a process of rapid thought.

He said, at last, 'I didn't realize you knew, Myra.' He had rejected prevarication it seemed.

'Oh, yes.'

She thought, and what's more, all of a sudden, out here, I know that I don't really love you any more. She watched him. He looked away. He pushed his plate aside, the food uneaten.

'Did you get her on the phone all right, just now?'

'It's the middle of the night, in England.'

'Of course – how silly of me. You could try this evening.'

'Please, Myra,' he said.

They sat in silence for a while. Myra finished her seafood salad, which was excellent. Many times, back home, in that other world where it was the middle of the night, she had thought about having this conversation but it had never, in the head, been at all like this.

'Myra . . .' he began.

She picked up the menu. 'Do you want a dessert? I'm having tropical fruit salad. Papaya, guava . . . What's pawpaw, do you know?'

He shook his head. 'Myra, I'm finding it hard to know what to say . . .'

'Never mind,' she said, quite kindly. 'You've had a shock.'

She observed him. Behind his head, the Blue Mountains smoothly revolved. His face had a shrivelled look; he sat hunched into his chair. It occurred to Myra that he had become slightly smaller within the last few minutes. He was a big man normally, who sat erect.

Her next words rose quite unconsidered to her lips. 'Do you want to get rid of me and marry her?'

As soon as she had spoken she saw that she had hit the jackpot. George's eyes were eloquent with panic.

'No. No, Myra. Absolutely not. The last thing I . . . Look, should we talk about all this here? Wouldn't it be better if we sat down quietly back at the hotel . . . Or maybe when we get home to England, when we've both had a chance to think a bit.'

'I've been thinking,' said Myra. 'Quite a bit, really. But you may be right. We'll leave it, then. Sure you don't want any dessert?'

They finished the meal. Not in silence, for Myra chatted of the scenery and of their fellow eaters and George, wearing still this strange diminished look, responded wanly to her comments. He agreed that the Japanese were obsessed with photography. He turned to note the grove of casuarinas that she pointed out. On the walk back to the coach he listened – fruitlessly – for the bellbird.

The driver stood by the door. He said to Myra, 'Hi, there,' and Myra smiled. The passengers resumed their seats, the coach started up and began the slow, twisting descent down from the unfettered vistas of the mountain ranges and into the neat and structured universe of the Hawkesbury River valley and the wide road to Sydney. The commentary ceased. A movie came on; headphones were distributed.

George sat holding his newspaper, but did not turn the pages. And Myra saw now that they would not talk, either at the hotel or back home in England. What had passed between them today would remain for ever beyond the Blue Mountains, potent and powerful. She felt a touch sorry for Bridget Cashell. And possibly for George.

The Children of Grupp

When Trevor Cartwright first saw the Medusa Fountain it was the nymphs who caught his attention. Naturally enough. He set down the wheelbarrow for a moment and had a good look; very nice too, all those luscious marble girls. It was his second day as trainee gardener at Rockwell Manor under the Youth Opportunities Programme. He was seventeen; he'd rather have been elsewhere; he wanted farm work, proper stuff with machinery, not messing about clipping hedges and sweeping up leaves.

The gardens of Rockwell Manor are renowned for topiary and statues. The Medusa Fountain, at the end of the famous Yew Walk, is of course the *pièce de résistance*. The Medusa, framed by ferns and the dripping grotto, presides over the great basin of the fountain, at the base of which a charming group of cherubs is arranged in frozen play. Around the rim of the basin sit or recline youthful naked figures – exquisite Apollos and the languid nymphs which appealed to Trevor. The Medusa herself is so encrusted with moss and lichen that she is barely recognizable as a face, while the snakes of her hair have long since fused with the background of rock and greenery. Trevor did not even see her, on that first occasion; in any case he did not like to hang around too long or he'd have Fletcher down on him like a ton of bricks. Fletcher was the head gardener, and a right so-and-so. That he was in fact a first cousin once removed of Trevor's did not qualify his brusque treatment of the newest YOP. So, having taken in the girls and the blokes and all those stone babies larking around in the cool green water – no bad place to be, on a sweltering August afternoon – Trevor lifted the wheelbarrow once more and set off towards his next task.

He knew the gardens well, of course. He'd been born and grown up a mile away. The hamlet of Grupp, a dour little collection of tied cottages, has traditionally supplied the labour force for the manor and its gardens, open to the public since the 1930s. Trevor's grandfather had worked there, and his great-grandfather before that. His own father had managed to break out, and got himself into the building trade when times were better. Now, the economic climate had forced Trevor back into the mould; resentfully, he had presented himself at the estate office. His mother, of a more subservient and less querulous generation, had told him off for being truculent: 'There's always been a to and fro between Grupp and the manor. They're funny people, the Saxbys, but they done all right by the village. Back in Grandad's day there was estate parties once a year – swimming in the fountain, for the children, and a skittle alley in the stable yard.' Trevor was unimpressed.

The present owner, Colonel Saxby, was a recluse, inflated

by local rumour to a vaguely sinister figure, for no reliable reason. The wider world certainly found him unaccommodating; art historians interested in the statuary were turned away with a handout to the effect that no records existed concerning the provenance of the various pieces and that photography was not allowed. The figures were of indeterminate age – most appeared to be vaguely eighteenth-century, though some of the draped classical ladies presiding over the Yew Walk might well have been earlier. The Medusa Fountain was a puzzle – those experts who had been able to inspect it closely felt that as a group it was not consistent: figures seemed to have been added at different times. Even the cherubs – the adorable children tumbling and laughing around the foot of the fountain itself – appeared to the practised eye to be slightly at odds with one another, some so worn by time that features and dimples had almost vanished, others with their smiles and marble curls still sharply sculptured.

The gardens did not, in fact, attract large numbers of visitors. Advertising was desultory; opening times were capricious. Of those who did come, most were struck by the melancholy atmosphere of the place, an atmosphere that seemed indeed to spill out into the surrounding countryside, so that the dark hedgerows and lowering copses became an extension of the brooding woodland and sombre rides of the manor gardens. Those who knew no better said that a few good herbaceous borders would have cheered the place up; others, more practised in earlier traditions of gardening, commented on its picturesque qualities but still felt a chill as they plodded down endless vistas between dank hedges from which stared the blank stone eyes of Dianas and Cupids and Apollos. If, on leaving the car park, they failed to take the turn that led back to the main road and fetched up by mistake in Grupp, the sense of gloom and abandonment would be reinforced. The cottages had a sullen look; there was neither shop nor pub. Appearance, indeed, was reinforced by reputation; Grupp people were said to keep themselves to themselves; there was gossip about inbreeding and absence of initiative. Certainly, the hamlet had today a semi-abandoned air; several of the cottages were in derelict condition. Aspiring purchasers from Birmingham or London were turned away at the estate office with a blunt refusal: estate cottages were never put on the market. A demographic historian, attracted by interestingly high infant mortality rates, was met with cold stares and slammed front doors.

Trevor, a child of Grupp, knew only that he yearned for a proper man's job with machinery – tractors and muck-spreaders and combines – instead of which here he was stuck in the gardens with a wheelbarrow and a rake and Fletcher bawling him out if he deviated from instructions for an instant. He found himself working in isolation for the most part, hand-weeding on his knees in remoter regions of the gardens, monotonously raking lawns, trundling barrowloads of debris to the compost heaps. It was a summer of relentless heat and humidity. Employees at Rockwell were required to dress decorously. On his first day Trevor had stripped to the waist, and was roundly abused by Fletcher; thereafter he sweated in his shirt and cast envious glances at the marble nudity all round him – the gleaming torsos, the pale curves of buttocks and breasts, the slender bared limbs. It was all a bit sexy, too, no question about it, could get you quite worked up when you were on your own with them – waving their arses at you from among the trees.

After his first brief glimpse of the Medusa Fountain Trevor found himself irresistibly drawn to the spot. He made several illicit detours that day, for the pleasure of a quick splash of the face and hands in the water. There was something gloomy about the place, that was undeniable, but the watery cool of it, and the silver splash of the fountain, compensated for the gloom, while he came to feel the figures positively companionable. One particular nymph became a favourite. There she sat, curled on the rim of the basin with her hand held shyly over her breasts, as though she had been caught out in a private skinny-dip. On first acquaintance he had found her arousing; now, after several visits, he looked at her differently, seeing her beautiful immobility as in some way sad and vulnerable. She seemed to have an expression of eternal shock and surprise in her blank stone eyes; there was a quality in her face that was familiar, too. To be honest, she had a look of his Auntie Marian. Even, ever so slightly, of his own mum.

He became bolder in his visits to the fountain. He lingered for longer, trailed his hands and arms in the water, sat on the rim of the basin for a minute or two, idly splashing. He was tempting providence and providence, inevitably, struck. He had dunked his face in the water and was vigorously sousing his hair when a voice made him spring guiltily upright. 'Take a dip then, boy. Go on. Get stripped off. No need to be ashamed of your body – you'd stand comparison with that lot, by the look of you!'

It was the Colonel. Couldn't be anyone else. There he stood, just below the Medusa head – short, stocky, tweed-suited, grinning from the ferns and rocks of the grotto. Creepy, sprung from nowhere like that.

'We're not allowed to,' stammered Trevor. 'We're not allowed to take us shirts off, even.'

'It'll be between you and me,' said the Colonel. 'Who's to know? Old Fletcher's busy in the greenhouses. You can take your time. Go on, boy – don't be a fool.' He bared his teeth at Trevor in what was apparently meant as a smile, and was gone. No wonder people said he was a peculiar old bastard.

Trevor looked around. It was quite true – Fletcher was occupied elsewhere. It was not a public opening day. He was quite alone. He hesitated, then ripped off his shirt, jeans and underpants and stepped into the fountain.

It was wonderful. Deliciously cool, and deeper than you would have thought. He was up to his waist. He waded around, revelling in it. He swam a few strokes. Then he rolled on his back and floated, blissfully, gazing up at the dappled ceiling of leaves that flickered across a pale blue sky. He could have stayed there for ever.

Wiser to cut short the risk, though. Better get going.

Reluctantly, he stood up, stepped to the edge, hauled himself out on to the rim and sat with his legs in the water to savour a last few delightful moments. The stone figures around him mirrored the contours of his own pink young body. He glanced, a touch complacently, at his lean torso, his flat muscular flanks, his long legs; what had the old bloke said about comparisons with that lot?

He looked across the pool at the grotto; the Medusa, snake-haired and mossy, stared straight at him. The light seemed to dim, as though the sun had gone in; the frolicking cherubs dulled from gold to grey. It wasn't so warm, either; he started to withdraw his legs from the water. They felt oddly stiff and leaden; maybe he'd got a bit of a cramp. He sat, trying to flex his toes; he seemed to have no sensation in them at all. He could see them, down there in the greenish water, as though they were someone else's.

He reached out for his shirt, lying on the barrow behind him, to give himself a rub down with it. At least, he tried to reach but now his arm too was numb, leaden, he could scarcely lift it. He hauled it an inch or two – and it fell back inert in his lap. Panic seized him: 'I'm ill!' he thought. 'I've had a heart attack, like Grandad – I'll die, sat here like this.' He tried to shout, and his jaw would not move. He dragged his hand up to his face, with hideous effort; he touched his mouth, saw his fist lie against it, and felt nothing.

He moved his head, inch by inch, fighting his own rigidity; he tried to look towards the great Yew Walk, to see if anyone might be within sight. He could not see that far, but he was looking now at his neighbour on the rim of the fountain, at the nymph, the girl, his favourite, she who shielded her breasts with one hand in eternal modesty. And her stone eyes met his, it seemed, not in shock or surprise but in terrible grief.

He saw the colour ebb from his own body. He saw the delicate veining of marble appear on his thighs. He saw himself become uniform with the nymphs, with Apollo, with the mermaid and the satyr, and with the cherubs – those plump children frozen in play at the foot of the fountain, their marble curls touched with golden lichen. Some while after all feeling had left him, when he knew himself to be no longer a creature of flesh and blood but an object deep within which there lurked some awful consciousness of what had once been – some time then he heard and saw the Colonel. He saw him come again and stand below the grotto, contemplating his possessions. But Trevor had lost all sense of time by then; it might have been the next day, or the next month or the next year. Time would cease to be for Trevor; the seasons would succeed one another as he remained locked within the prison of his fine young body. The snow would lie in ridges along his arms, heap up on his thighs and fill his lap. The summer sun would bake him. The autumn leaves would pile up around him and float on to the surface of the water. He would hear the voices of visitors, the blank globes of his eyes would register their passage – bright moving blurs of colour beyond the rigid presences of his companions, suspended in time, locked in a dreadful eternity of weather and memory. There they would sit and recline, the handsome youths, the graceful girls. And the cherubs . . . oh, but the thought of the children of Grupp is beyond bearing.

The Slovenian Giantess

'Definitely you must see this castle,' said Eva. 'It is very historic.'

The rain fell in thick curtains. They had driven up a narrow, twisting road down which water gushed. Eva drove leaning forward to peer through the streaming windscreen. They were now in the castle car park, ostensibly waiting for a break in the weather. Eleanor had proposed that they abandon the venture and go for lunch in the hotel down below, by the lake.

'No, no. The castle is essential. What is some rain!' Eva laughed. 'In England it never stops raining, I thought. I was in London last year to work at the British Library and it was every day – rain, rain, rain.'

'There are occasional periods of respite,' said Eleanor.

Eva opened the car door. 'Come on. We must be brave. It is not so far to walk, I think.'

The castle perched on the highest point of the crags that reared above one shore of the lake. Seen from down below, jutting out of the pinkish-grey rock and the dark mantle of trees, it looked like some carefully considered scenic device, a set piece for the enjoyment of observers in the recently constructed lakeside resort complex – hotels, restaurants, conference centre and boutiques. Eva and Eleanor, walking awkwardly close together in order to share an umbrella, stumbled up the stony path that led to the castle entrance. There was no one else about; the car park had been empty.

'Maybe it's shut,' said Eleanor.

'No, no. Always these places are open.' There was a big wooden door set into the outer wall of the castle precinct at which Eva now hammered.

Rain crashed on to the umbrella. After a minute or so a custodian appeared, looking surprised, and watched without interest the ritual scuffle over who was to pay.

'I am the hostess,' said Eva firmly. 'In England, another time, it will be your turn.'

This was what Eleanor feared. Eva was a lecturer at the University of Zagreb and Eleanor was not sure that she liked her that much. Around forty, a few years older than herself, Eva was a somewhat frenzied woman with a mane of wiry black hair and a professional interest in anglophone women writers of the early twentieth century. She had battened on to Eleanor throughout the three days of the conference. This expedition to the lake on the final afternoon was at her insistence. The concluding sessions left Eleanor with four hours to spare before check-in time for her flight back to London. When Eva discovered this she had proposed a trip to the mountain lake. 'You will have your luggage with you and then I take you straight to the airport.'

Eleanor had demurred, partly on account of a certain lack of enthusiasm for Eva's company, but also because it was clear that a longish drive would be involved. By that time the countdown to departure would have begun and the airport would be exercising its magnetic pull. She had not much faith in Eva's time sense, or indeed in her battered little car. She had made excuses, but Eva would have none of it. 'You don't trust me, Eleanor. You think I will not get you to your plane.' And so decency had required a gracious acceptance and now here they were, plodding round the ramparts of this gothic monument in the father and mother of all downpours with the lake below barely visible through grey veils of rain. Never mind, thought Eleanor, never mind. All part of life's rich pattern. By 6.30 I'll be on BA 354 to Heathrow. Home by eleven, with any luck.

'Ah,' said Eva. 'Here is the entrance. Now we go in and get dry. In England of course you have plenty of castles. I should like next year to do a trip. Perhaps we go together and you will be my guide.'

They toured the rooms. The furnishings were tapestries, much stricken with age, and vast blackened cupboards, tables and settles. There were some perfunctory showcases of china, coins and objets d'art. Eva translated the explanatory leaflet. 'Yes, this is very historic. From the eleventh century, with many rebuildings. Where we are now is from the seventeenth. Here is the fine view of the lake. And it is raining not so much now.'

They looked over a cliff face down which Serbs and Croats

had apparently been throwing one another for hundreds of years. The castle's past, inextricably entwined with that of the region, was characterized by violence and implacable tribal feuding. It had changed hands each century, it seemed, to the accompaniment of further slaughter. Eleanor, contemplating the grey-black water, the sweeping pine forests and rain-sodden rocks, had a feeling of being in the bloodstained heartlands of Europe with history hanging like some dreadful miasma of pollution.

Eva's footsteps came clattering back from the next room. 'Come – here is something most interesting.'

In the centre of the room was an oblong wooden pen of sand on which lay a huge skeleton. 'Here is the skeleton of the Slovenian giantess,' said Eva. 'She is from the tenth century, it says. And beside her is her necklace and the head-dress she wore.'

'Heavens – she certainly was tall! Seven foot, do you think?'

'We will see. I am five foot eight.' Eva got down and lay on the floor alongside the skeleton. Eleanor stood and looked at them both – the immense bony frame of this survivor of the tenth century and Eva, a Croat of the twentieth. Eva lay there, her arms stiff at each side of her, in a dark blue double-breasted coat with brass buttons and knee boots with high heels, still clutching her handbag. 'Well?' she said.

Eleanor was quite disoriented by the sight. She stared down.

'Well?' said Eva again. 'Is she seven feet?'

'At least. A bit more, I'd say.'

Eva got up and dusted herself off. 'And now definitely the rain is not so bad, so we will drive to the hotel for lunch. And we will talk about where I can apply for a study grant in England next year.'

Yes, thought Eleanor, I suppose that is what we're here for, if the truth were told. No, that's a disgraceful thought. She is merely being hospitable to a visitor.

Given the choice, it was not Eva with whom she would have struck up an acquaintance. Indeed it could be said that Eva had scuppered her chances with the one appealing man of around her own age on the conference, a Henry James scholar from Sarajevo called Boris. Every conference has its Lothario and Boris was probably that, a fact of which Eleanor had been well aware, but in the artificial circumstances of three-day cloistered proximity, who cares? Boris had been drily entertaining and initially distinctly attentive, but every time she found herself with him Eva hove in sight with cries of greeting and muscled in on the conversation, killing it stone dead. Boris, tilting a sardonic eyebrow, would drift away.

The conference was a biennial forum on English literature studies held by teachers of the subject in Yugoslavian universities. Eleanor herself was one of only half a dozen British delegates, included presumably to leaven the mixture. Everyone else knew one another rather too well. She had given her paper on Virginia Woolf and then settled into the audience in the Hall of Culture presided over by a relentlessly autocratic professor from the host university. 'No speaker will address the conference for more than thirty minutes please. We will then have twenty minutes for discussion and five minutes for concluding remarks from the chair . . .' Eleanor had listened to presentations on 'The Macedonian response to the Movement poets' and 'The Serbo-Croat reception of the Sirens episode in *Ulysses*' and the event had come to seem more and more surreal. For outside the lecture hall no one talked of anything but the patently more compelling matter of the imminent break-up of Yugoslavia.

'You must understand that Yugoslavia is not a country but a cultural salad,' said Boris, on the first occasion that they talked. 'Is this your first visit?'

It was. She felt humiliated by her ignorance, by the assorted fragments of information that stood in for knowledge or understanding of this place and of these people. What she heard bore no resemblance to the dispassionate accounts of newspaper reports. She felt her own detachment from their concerns and with it an unsettling guilt, as though she were watching distant wars on a television screen.

And then on the second morning Eva came into the breakfast room and made straight for her. 'I have some bad news for you, Eleanor. Your Mrs Thatcher is defeated.'

Eleanor stared. It was early in the morning, she had slept badly and the domestic political situation was far from her mind.

'She is not any longer the prime minister. She is thrown out.'

'Oh, good,' said Eleanor.

Eva was astonished. 'But this is surely very bad for your country. She is a great leader.'

Boris had just brought Eleanor another cup of coffee. He sat down.

'Well, some of us don't feel that,' said Eleanor.

Boris laughed.

'Anyway, this is what has happened.' Eva shrugged. 'It is the first item on the news, before even what the Serbs are saying. And I cannot see what is so funny, Boris. For Eleanor this is a very historical moment.'

'Ah, but Eleanor does not feel that it is,' said Boris. 'History is a question of perspective, I suppose. The downfall of Mrs Thatcher will not much affect Eleanor's life.'

Eva helped herself to one of Eleanor's pieces of bread. 'Do you mind? I will get more in a minute. Boris is being clever – you should pay no attention.'

'Actually I think he's right,' said Eleanor. 'It's the difference between our politics and . . . those in other places.'

'Such as here,' – Boris gave Eva a bland smile and addressed himself to Eleanor – 'where we may be about to be exposed to rather more history than we would like. Usually history is what happens somewhere else and at some other time. It should be avoided at all costs, or kept at a low temperature, as you manage to do in England.'

Eva snorted. 'This is a very silly conversation, I think. Are you coming for the dinner at the Greek restaurant tonight, Eleanor? We could then talk some more about my article on Virginia Woolf's feminism.'

At which point Boris had slid away, with a regretful little grimace at Eleanor.

And now here she was, crammed into Eva's car, hurtling around this menacing landscape on a day of intermittent cloudbursts, already in her mind slotted once more into her own life, picking up the letters on the doormat (there wouldn't be many – she'd only been away four days), unpacking the case, thinking about the week ahead. It was still term time – she had a heavy teaching load and had had to cancel two seminars and a lecture in order to get to this conference. She considered ways of making these up, as the car plunged down the narrow road to the lakeside.

'This hotel is built quite recently,' said Eva. 'It is all newly laid out. They are hoping to attract foreign tourists and conferences.'

The entire lakeside resort had a doleful air of incompletion and abandonment. The pedestrian shopping precinct was a miniature townscape of empty windows and unpeopled walkways. The skating-rink and putting-green were closed. There was hardly anyone around. Eva led Eleanor into the hotel, which was equally deserted. They made their way through vast lounges in which oversized sofas and chairs bleakly confronted one another, and thence into a dining-room, one wall of which was a great sheet of glass overlooking the lake. Waiters wearing tuxedos converged upon them, proffering wine lists and urging them to make their selection from the cold buffet at the other side of the room.

Surveying this spread, Eleanor was again seized with a sense of the surreal. Whole salmon garnished with skewered twists of cucumber and lemon. Other cold fish, piped with rosettes of mayonnaise. Ranks of different kinds of salad, platters of sliced meats. Little bowls of caviare on ice.

'All for us?'

'Perhaps they are expecting some conference,' said Eva. 'Here maybe we will share the bill, shall we? Go Dutch – is that right?'

They returned to their table with heaped plates. The weather had improved and the lake was fully visible now, dimpled by light rain, sweeping away to a dark, distant backcloth of trees. Eleanor felt disembodied, only tenuously present, on loan to this place for a few hours, courtesy of British Airways. She had felt much like that throughout the conference. Occasionally the map of Europe would form itself in her head. She would see the familiar outline, pay tribute to the distances. This place was nearly a thousand miles from London, but of course it was not that. It was as far as the half-hour in the airport and the wander round the duty-free shops, the three-hour flight with the read of the papers and a book, the meal, the brief doze. That was the reality, not this eerie sense of an elsewhere in which she was present only as a transitory ghost. In dreams, you can experience that sense of licence – this is only a dream and therefore I can do as I wish and cannot be brought to book.

She was here in the same spirit. Prick her and she would not bleed.

Perhaps that is why people behave out of character as soon as they leave their own country, she thought. Have love affairs with Italian waiters, sleep around at conferences. She had not herself done either of these things but it did occur to her now that her resistance might not have been so great had Boris become pressing. Under normal circumstances she liked to take her time about sexual commitment, so this perception was interesting. She even felt a mild regret. She glanced at her watch. Only two and a half hours now till check-in time.

Eva was talking about her family. Her widowed mother in Zagreb. Her brother who had a successful import and export business, threatened now by the impending collapse of Yugoslavia.

A word, thought Eleanor, just a word. You can't make a country out of a word. And for her, she realized, this place was a preconception built around that word – present in the mind as an arbitrary sequence of images. A ragged procession of refugee women and children following the partisans into the mountains. These mountains? Tito – a stocky figure with shiny boots, crammed into a uniform that bristled with epaulettes and buttons, a grin like the Cheshire cat. Derring-do British officers parachuting into the partisan camps – Randolph Churchill, Evelyn Waugh. As irrelevant surely as the Sirens episode in *Ulysses*. Sarajevo. The Archduke Ferdinand. The single shot that plunged Europe into war, or so one understood. None of this had any connection with the acreage of white napery around her, the bored waiters, the lake with its torrential pine forests, the castle of the Slovenian giantess.

Eva was now talking of an uncle, her mother's brother, who had emigrated to the United States immediately after the war and had recently returned on a visit, for the first time. A dismaying visit, it emerged.

'Eleanor, he did not even speak good English,' Eva confided. 'After forty years over there. He has been always with an enclave of Croatian émigrés in Cleveland, working just as a garage mechanic. My mother was . . . embarrassed by him. His manners. His way of speaking. My family is quite different now. My mother was head teacher of a big school. My brother is well known in business. But he was . . . well, from another world. He was twenty-one when he left. And still all he can talk about is the war. The war, the war, the war. For us it is long ago now, the war. It is finished, done with. He has mended cars in Cleveland all his life and thought of nothing but the war, him and his friends.'

'Why did he emigrate?'

'There were problems for some people, back then. Others trying to settle old scores. You know . . . He did not feel safe. They said he had some connection with the Ustashi.'

'Did he?'

'I don't know,' Eva shrugged. 'If so . . . he was very young. But the point is, all that is gone now, for people like us. Finished. We have moved on. But he had not. In the end it was hard to talk to him. My mother was relieved when he went back to the States.'

'Had you met him when you were doing your doctorate over there?'

'No, no,' said Eva, a trifle irritably. 'I was in Pittsburgh. It would have been much too far to visit him.'

Their plates had been removed and the waiters were now trying to interest them in the dessert trolley. Eva abandoned her family and wrenched the conversation firmly in the direction of her own prospects of a research grant at a British university. Eleanor had a certain satisfaction in explaining that the Thatcher years had made such largesse hard to come by. She promised to make inquiries.

The meal completed, Eva made a meticulous division of the bill and looked at her watch. 'Excellent – we have still plenty of time. I shall take you to see the waterfall.'

'Well . . . maybe I should be getting straight to the airport now.'

'No, no. You will only be sitting about there – it is half an hour from here, that is all. And the waterfall is not to be missed. We can drive to a place not far away and then it is a short walk up the mountainside. I have been many times.'

The road climbed up from the lake even more tortuously than that to the castle, doubling back on itself in hairpin bends. It was not much more than a track, in any case. The rain had given way now to a thickening mist.

Eleanor said, 'Is this where the partisans were, in the war?'

'Probably. They were in many places. Certainly near here is where there was a massacre by the Germans, I think. Look, this now is where we leave the car.'

'It's going to start getting dark soon, Eva. Are you sure it isn't far?'

'Not far at all. This is the way over here, look . . . It is a well-known beauty spot.'

But not in the middle of November, thought Eleanor dourly. It was distinctly chilly now and the air was thick with moisture. She tied her scarf round her head and followed Eva up the steep shaly path, slippery from the rain, which wound up between the trees. Eva, in her high-heeled boots, was having difficulty. Eleanor, pointing this out in hopes of a reprieve, was brushed aside. At any moment they would reach the waterfall, Eva assured her. 'Hush . . . I think I can hear it already.'

For nearly twenty minutes they scrambled up the mountainside. Then Eva stopped. 'It is possible I have taken the wrong path. I think perhaps we go down some way and see if we have missed a turn.'

Eleanor said, 'I really do feel it would be wise to head for the airport now, Eva.'

'No, no. We are very close, I promise.' Turning, Eva began a hasty and hazardous descent. Within half a dozen paces she had fallen. Her left foot slipped and twisted and she was on her back on the rain-sodden path.

It was quickly apparent that damage had been done. As soon as Eva tried to get up she became faint. Eleanor squatted beside her on the path, supporting her. 'Just keep still for a minute. You've probably winded yourself.'

'I am all right. Look, I can get up now . . .' But there was a yelp of pain. 'My ankle . . .'

'Keep still,' said Eleanor. She improvised a pillow with their two handbags and unzipped Eva's boot. 'Does that hurt?'

It did. And the ankle was beginning to swell. Broken or merely sprained?

'I try to stand,' said Eva. 'Look, it is not so bad . . .' And immediately fainted.

Eleanor ministered. She found some skin freshener in her handbag and rubbed it on Eva's forehead. Oh God, she thought, what a thing to happen . . . Presently Eva came to. She stared at Eleanor. 'I am not so good. You will have to take the car and go to get some help. Here – the keys are in my pocket.'

'Eva,' said Eleanor, 'I'm afraid I can't drive.' And have always rather prided myself on the fact, she reflected grimly. Felt myself a touch radical, original. Environmentally chaste.

Eva closed her eyes. 'Ah . . .' She opened them. 'I am afraid that you may miss your plane.'

'That's the least of it,' said Eleanor heroically. 'The main thing is to get you down from here. Let's try once more and see if you might be able to walk if you lean on me and we take it very slowly.'

They tried. Eva all but passed out again.

'I'm going to have to leave you and find some help,' said Eleanor. Hell and damnation, she thought. Shit. She saw the airport departure lounge, the reassuring departure board: BA354 London Heathrow. The light blinking: BOARDING.

'I made perhaps a mistake to go to the waterfall,' said Eva. 'I am sorry, Eleanor. This is most inconvenient for you.' She was now extremely white.

'Never mind. Now look – can you wriggle as far as that pile of leaves there? You'd be a bit more comfortable.'

Eva was laid out by the side of the path. For the second time Eleanor stood looking down at the woman's supine form – the buttoned coat, those boots, her now ashen face. I knew this would happen, thought Eleanor, somehow I knew it. It was built into the day from the moment we walked into that castle. But it is not a major catastrophe. Eva's injury is a minor one. I have missed a plane, that is all. What I have to do is follow the path and then the road. Sooner or later there'll be a car. The driver of which probably won't speak any English.

She tore a page from a notebook on which Eva wrote a message of explanation and appeal. She still looked extremely seedy but was rallying sufficiently to instruct Eleanor on a quicker way down from the car park. 'The road will take so long, and there will be no cars coming up here now. There is a path from where we left the car, for people who walk up to the waterfall. It is steep but much more quick, down to the big road where there will surely be cars.'

Eleanor hesitated. 'Well, I'll see how dark it's getting by the time I'm at the car park.'

'Do not fall . . .' came Eva's voice, as she departed.

Eleanor achieved the car park within ten minutes. And there indeed was the suggested path, with a wooden sign indicating the lakeside village. Clearly this would be a much quicker route than the tortuous hairpin bends of the road. The path looked definite enough, if a trifle steep, and it was still only early dusk.

After a few minutes of somewhat precipitate descent the path became rather less well defined, encroached on by undergrowth. Not much used, it would seem. Eleanor considered turning back. But then, after another minute or so, she found herself confronted by a bifurcation, one arm of which opened up in a distinctly more promising way and must surely be the descent to the main road. To go back now would be to lose a lot of time.

This branch of the path was steeper yet. Now and again she had to cling on to overhanging branches to steady herself. Good thing she had flat shoes on, not ludicrous boots like poor Eva. She glanced at her watch: 5.45. Check-in 6.15. Not a hope in hell.

It was distinctly murky now. And the path was getting more and more precipitous. I don't like this, she thought. This is crazy, I should have stuck to the road. The image in her head was the nirvana of the airport lounge, the reality which had somehow been snatched from her and replaced by this unpleasant, wet and darkening mountainside.

She struggled on. And now, to her horror, the path forked again. One route wound off to the left, the other continued steeply downwards. Oh God – which? Damn you, Eva – I should never have let you land me with this bloody path.

The path leading down seemed the most logical route, if the least inviting. Steeper and steeper. She was constantly slipping and sliding now. Trees closed in around her. The light was fading all the time.

She slithered down and down. The path began to level off. Eleanor's spirits rose – the road could not be far. The trees were too thick to see ahead, but at any moment they would surely start to thin out. She listened hopefully for cars.

Instead, there came the sound of rushing water. The forest did indeed thin out – to show a fast-flowing stream, into which the path led, to emerge on the other side and rise up a further tree-hung hillside. She had descended into a gully rather than to the road.

Her stomach was churning. It would be dark within fifteen minutes or so. She knew that she was starting to panic. Think, she told herself. *Think* what to do. To go back the way she had come was the safest in the sense that she was bound to end up back at the car park, but this would involve a horribly steep climb in darkness (why the hell didn't I ask Eva if there was a torch in her car?). The way ahead was unpredictable but considerably less steep. It seemed likely that the gully was just a fold in the hillside and that the path would yet descend to the road. The stream was narrow enough to jump.

She would go on.

When it was so dark that she could barely see ahead at all she knew with awful certainty that she had made the wrong decision. She should be at the road by now and was not. The path had climbed, and then began a reassuring descent, but now it was climbing once more. It was raining again. She was wet, exhausted and nearing despair. At one point she lost the path when undergrowth swept across it, and she realized only just in time that she had started to plunge off into the forest. She scrambled on with her eyes all the time on the faintly pale surface of the stony track. She no longer thought of the comforting interior of BA 354, where she should rightly be. Occasionally she saw Eva lying on a pile of leaves in the dark somewhere above and beyond. Once when she peered at her watch she realized that she had been walking now for over an hour. She was dizzy with fatigue and when she seemed to hear a horde of shuffling feet around her she thought that she was hallucinating until the sound turned to the drip of water from the trees above. But the sense of unreality that she had experienced over the last few days was gone. She knew now that she was here, in this place, on this implacable hillside, hundreds of miles from home and that there was no bland assurance of stepping back into her own life. She understood that reality is what is happening to you, not what you anticipate. She perceived also, with a clarity she had never known, that there are realities which for most of us are beyond imagination.

And with this perception came fear – fear such as she had never known, fear that seemed to come pouring from the trees to snatch her up and take her stumbling on and on into the wet whispering darkness. She was invaded by fear, a fear beyond all reason. She knew only that she had to go on – to go on and to get away. She no longer thought of the plane, she no longer thought of Eva, only of her own desperate plight and this terrible shroud of trees that closed in on her and from which she would never escape.

Later that night, much later, an electrician returning home after a drinking session with a friend was puzzled to see a stumbling swaying figure by the side of the road. A woman. A woman with a scarf tied round her head. For a moment he felt a creep of unease and superstition, as though something of another time might have come crawling from these forests in which, everyone knew, dark things had come about. And then he saw that she was waving and shouting and he pulled up alongside, wound down the window and heard her gabble incomprehensibly. It was one o'clock in the morning, his mind was on his own warm bed and the wife who would want to know where the devil he had been. This sodden figure weaving about in the mist seemed like some effect of the drinks he'd put down, but when she thrust a piece of paper at him he took it and peered at the scrawl. Then he gestured the woman into the passenger seat, turned the van round and headed for the road to the waterfall, while his passenger sat there shivering.

'And how did you and your friend get yourselves into this fix?' he inquired, not unkindly. But all the woman would do was shake her head and mutter, an alien apparition sprung from the night.

In Olden Times

She lived by the clock. Her days were apportioned, hour by hour, parcelled up into time at work, time for sleeping, time for house cleaning, for shopping, time for the children. An hour, a half-hour, ten minutes. Time for love-making; time for ironing, for cooking, for taking a bath. A crisis meant time borrowed from one sector and forever owed – the entire week flung out of order by an emergency visit to the surgery, or a faulty washing-machine or car that would not start. And each day was punctuated by the rigorous, inescapable blasts of the whistle: 7.30 (evening) – leave for work; 8.45 (morning) – arrive home from work; 8.50 – Tim leaves for work. Take children to school; sleep till 1; clean, wash, shop, fetch children from school. Attend to children – laugh, chat, listen. Glimpse, for a moment, the parallel but alien universe in which the girls live, Katie and Linda, aged seven and eight, a place in which time was pliable, wayward, in which an hour could be a day, the clock could stop still or whirl unrestrained, in which you could be quite unfettered by chronology, stepping from moment to moment, not knowing if it were morning or afternoon.

'It's all rush, rush, rush with you people nowadays,' said old Mrs Arthur, her regular patient. 'When I was your age we took life as it came. We didn't try to cram forty-eight hours into twenty-four. Going to give me a bath tonight, Marion, are you?'

She was an agency nurse and worked nights; Tim, her husband, was an accountant, and worked days. They passed each other twice daily, like ferries plying to and from a harbour. On Saturday nights she did not work, and they made love, luxuriously. Sometimes they had a quick go mid-week too, in between Tim getting home and her leaving – in haste with the bedroom door locked while the girls were watching telly.

She did sums in her head, continuously – as she drove, as she peeled potatoes, as she brushed her hair or cleaned her teeth. The mortgage plus the insurance plus the electricity the gas the telephone the holiday money. Tim's salary plus my pay. Five hundred and ninety-six in the building society. The housekeeping plus the children's dinner money plus the boiler repair bill plus Katie's new shoes. Figures flew around inside her head, neat in columns, plus or minus, or jumbled and spinning, unrestrained and unstoppable.

'Never satisfied,' said old Mrs Arthur. 'That's what's wrong with people today. Videos and those computer things and I don't know what. I had a three-piece when I got married, and a new gas cooker, and thought I was well off. Now it's want, want, want.'

She made the girls a dolls' house out of a tea-chest –

anguished secret hours with plywood and saw and hammer and tacks and battered fingers. Wallpaper remnants, carpet offcuts and real pictures on the walls, in tiny photograph frames. She was the good mother. All right, so they didn't have holidays in Spain or Greece, but they had a dolls' house. They had a mother who fetched them from school, who helped them with their homework, who paid attention.

'We're learning about the olden days this term,' they told her. 'Old-fashioned times. The Victorian times. We're going to do a project. And we're going to have a Victorian day and it'll be a Victorian school and we'll be children in old-fashioned times.'

'Goodness!' she said. 'Well!'

There was always a half-hour missing in the day, somehow – mislaid, gone astray. At night, at Mrs Arthur's, cat-napping in a sleeping-bag on the couch, getting up two-hourly to check the patient, she would still feel out of breath, as though she had run a race and failed to keep up.

She was a State Registered Nurse. She knew many things; she had many skills. She could inject and dress and dose; she could lift and turn, fetch and carry. She could alleviate pain; she could save life. She could also sand floors and strip walls and hang paper and apply paint or distemper. She could change a washer or fit a plug. She could cut hair, make a soufflé, assemble within fifteen minutes and without notice the materials with which to construct a rag doll like children had in olden times, to take to school tomorrow morning.

Everyone's got to bring one, Mum, so can we do it now, before tea?

Tim went to evening classes to learn car maintenance and thus save on garage bills. He was not a technically competent person, not the sort of man who is always about the place with spirit-level and power drill, who swarms confidently up stepladders. He would peer disconsolately into the car's innards, the manual in his hand, frowning and fiddling. She felt an ache of pity, and wanted to help, but knew she would probably do no better. The car was a tyrant, and a saviour. It gobbled money, lost value, would eventually have to be replaced; and they could not do without it. Should it break down, then the whole delicate precise time table of the day was destroyed – laid waste by long waits for buses, the trudge across town to the children's school or to the shops. As she drove, she was always on edge for those ominous little sounds – a squeak, a rattle, an alien note to the engine, the heralds of disaster. The car was five years old, vulnerable, on the brink of decline. She was locked into hatred of it, and dependence, as in some stale habitual marriage.

'You've lost the use of your legs, you young people,' said Mrs Arthur. 'I walked two miles to school when I was a child, two there and two back. And when I was a working girl I'd take the tram. We never thought to drive a car, back then.'

On Mondays and Wednesdays and Fridays she went to Mrs Arthur, who was semi-paralysed after a stroke. Mrs Arthur's daughter, who coped for the rest of the week, thus achieved three nights at home with her family. Marion would have a quick chat with the daughter in the hall, coming and going: two women in a hurry, in tacit complicity, knowing with unerring insight what the other's life was like, so that they could talk in shorthand – a coded exchange about children, and time and money and the way of the world. Colluding, buoying one another up.

On the other nights she worked at a geriatric nursing home, in twilit wards filled with sighing and coughing and the sudden authoritative tap of footsteps as the duty nurses attended to a call or a crisis.

In the mornings, at home, when she slept in her own room with the curtains drawn and the windows outlined by a hard edge of light from the insistent day beyond, voices from the street would invade her dreams, as she cruised just below the level of consciousness. Inhabiting that surreal dream world in which there is no logic, in which time is not sequential but episodic, in which anything is possible, she would hear the voices as nagging or peremptory reminders of an elsewhere, filling her with unease, with the sense that there was something she should be doing, somewhere she should be going. And then she would wake, subject at once to the tyrannous schedule of the day.

In Victorian times, the children reported, people worked in factories all day long, little children too. All day in horrid black rooms and they never played in the sunshine and they didn't go to school or learn anything. If you'd been born then you might have worked down a coalmine, Mum, pulling a cart like horses did. Honestly. Their eyes blazed with indignation. It wasn't all lovely in olden times, like people think, they told her.

She was happy, she believed. In fact she knew that she was happy. Occasionally – when she had a moment – she counted her blessings, as her mother used to advocate. Tim, the girls. All of them in good health. The house, the car, the washing-machine. She considered the house, which was like many, many other houses. Well, yes – the house was a blessing. Plenty of people do not have any house at all. The car, the washing-machine? Well, up to a point.

Just occasionally, she was able to identify happiness. She saw it made manifest, and perceived what it was. It was Linda belting towards her from the school gates, it was Katie laughing in the bath, it was Tim's face when they made love. It could be quite other things, too, quite different things – a blue and green May morning, starlight, the sun on your face. You could identify it – with hindsight, it always seemed. What you could not do was cost it, count it, add or subtract it. Catch and keep it. Interestingly, it seemed to have little to do with cars or washing-machines or, indeed, houses.

'When I was young,' said Mrs Arthur, 'there was none of this pollution. We had proper countryside, back then, with flowers and birds, and you could walk the length of the High Street without seeing a car. And there were real summers, back then, with sunshine end to end. No need to go traipsing off in aeroplanes to get a suntan.'

'And they made little boys be chimney-sweeps,' said Katie

and Linda. 'They sent them up hot chimneys and sometimes they got stuck. And lots of children died of illnesses because there was dirty water and they didn't have good food and baby clinics. And it was all smoky and smelly and foggy. But when we have our Victorian day it's not going to be like that. We're going to pretend it's an old-fashioned school like lucky children went to, and we're going to dress up and be the children.'

'Well!' she said. 'What fun!'

Each day was a course that she had to negotiate. She would look along the channel of the hours, each morning, with narrowed eyes, calculating the hazards, the tricky bends. Sometimes she had a clear run. On other days she stumbled her way through, betrayed by each obstacle, prey to a malign confederacy of ailing children, failed machinery, missing car keys. All days were the same, and entirely different.

Time was hours, which added up to days, and days which clustered to become a week. She saw it as an element, like air or water. The element in which she moved, through which she fought her way.

'Scrub my back, dear, would you?' said Mrs Arthur. And she would rub the flannel down skin that was flabby here and papery there, quite different from the plump, springy surfaces of her children. She always had her hands on bodies, it seemed – she was an expert on the smooth feel of thighs, the protuberance of feet, the way a breast hangs or a buttock curves. She could date flesh at a glance: time incarnate.

All days were the same, and different, and then every now

46

and then there would arrive a day that was in a class of its own, that pointed up the nature of all her days. Such as the day before the Victorian Day.

Which began like any other.

'Off now, are you?' said Mrs Arthur, barely awake, squinting up bleary from the bedclothes. 'I'll see you when I see you, then. Take care. Give yourself a break, you need it.'

It was crafty, that day. It pulled its punches, to start with. No traffic jam at the bridge, for once, green lights all the way down the High Street, home seven minutes earlier than usual. Time for a cup of tea with Tim; time to sew a button on Katie's shirt before school.

Then the day began to snarl. Rain, bucketing down. Katie falling in a puddle outside the school – mud-splashed, weeping.

She decided to shop on the way home, get that done. She weathered the check-out line, achieved the cashier, watched her pile rung up, groped for her purse – and knew then that she had left it on the seat of the car after finding the coin for the meter. A set-back, but relatively low on the scale of things – just a low hurdle, a treacherous bend in the road. (Leave shopping stacked at check-out; fetch purse from car; lose twenty minutes and forfeit ten-minutes-with-paper-and-cup-of-coffee when back at the house.)

But, back at the house, the day had its fangs properly bared. She put the washing in the machine, switched on, and water promptly gushed all over the floor. Inspection revealed a rotted lining. She removed the washing from the machine, dried the floor and rang repair firms, none of which could come till the day after tomorrow. She did the washing by hand. By now it was a quarter to twelve and she knew that she would not get her morning nap that day. Well, all right. Not the first time, and she had snoozed last night, on and off, between getting up to check old Mrs Arthur, turn her, take her the bed-pan. The mid-morning coffee she had not had could become an early lunch break. She put the kettle on.

The kettle remained cold and silent. She checked the plug, the switch: no progress. Now she felt that surge of impotent anger that had to be resisted, that got you nowhere. She fetched the screwdriver, dismantled the plug and found a blown fuse.

And no, of course there was not a spare fuse in the drawer where such things as spare fuses should be.

She weighed up the choices: get in car, drive to High Street, search for parking space, etc., or walk to corner shop which may or may not stock fuses. Fifteen—twenty minutes and certain fuse against four minutes and very possibly no fuse. She decided to live dangerously and gamble.

But lo, suddenly the day had relented, gone soft, turned a blind eye on her! For the corner shop did indeed have fuses — 3 amp, 5 amp, take your pick.

Back home, she set about installing the fuse and re-assembling the plug (on no account mislay tiny screws, which would never again be found). The cup of coffee was now within sight.

The phone rang. A neighbour, whose toddler has fallen and gashed his forehead; an edge of panic to her voice . . . 'I don't know if I should take him to the Casualty or not, could you come and have a look, Marion, sorry to ask but . . .'

Abandon plug (put screws in empty matchbox). Hasten to neighbour's house.

The gash is not disastrous but warrants a precautionary visit to the Casualty. And of course the child's mother has no car to hand so the only neighbourly course is to offer to drive her there. 'Really it's no bother. I've got a couple of hours at least before I have to get the girls from school.' (No – revise that – a half hour has evaporated since last she checked her watch. An hour and a half.)

A rough passage to the hospital: traffic jam in the High Street, a lorry unloading in what should have been a nifty short cut, the toddler fretting and the mother agitated. At last she got to the Casualty, saw them to the reception desk, set off home. But now she was not in good shape: that muzzy feeling in the head, heart going a little too hard and too fast, limbs fizzing as though lightly aerated. Calm down, Marion. Slow up; take it easy. But it was nearly a quarter to three now, and the girls must be picked up at half past. Also, there was something odd about the car, was there not? A dragging feel, a wobble to the steering.

She made it to the house, with sinking stomach to add to the leaden head and aerated limbs. Pull yourself together, Marion, it's only a flat tyre.

Only.

Scurry, now. Five to three, and she will have to walk to the main road, wait possibly ten minutes for the bus. She should make it to the school gates in time, but gone is the chance for that cup of coffee and the planned quick preparation of vegetables for the evening meal.

Twelve minutes, not ten, at the bus-stop. The girls already outside the school when she arrived. More walking, more waiting, more bus. Home at 4.20. Ah well.

And then it happened. 'Oh . . .' they said. 'Oh, Mum, it's the Victorian Day tomorrow. Didn't we tell you? Well, it is. And we're all to have mob caps and pinafores. You can make them out of old sheets, Mrs Sanderson says. You cut out a round, Mum, and machine it round the edge and then pull it up round the middle and it makes a frilly mob cap. It's easy-peasy. And you make the pinnies like this – look, she's drawn a pattern. And she said if your mum hasn't got a machine tell her she can just hem them round. OK? Mum?'

They gaze at her happily – excited, trusting.

'I see,' she says. 'Yes. Well. I wish you'd told me this yesterday. Or the day before.'

'Sorry, Mum,' they said. 'We forgot. We thought we had.'

So . . . Quick search of the airing-cupboard, to find a sheet old enough to be condemned. Get out the ancient Singer, once her mother's, which has not been used for many a long year, since she decided in early youth that dressmaking was not for her. At least the girls are tranquil elsewhere, busy on some concern of their own. One can get on unimpeded.

She cut out circles for the caps, squares for the pinnies.

So far, so good. But, oh God, a cup of tea would be a help! That bloody plug. It won't take a moment to fix it.

'Katie! You haven't touched the matchbox I left on the kitchen table, have you?'

The matchbox is now incorporated into a sofa that they are making for the dolls' house. Hence the tranquillity. The screws? They gaze at her again, in guilt and anxiety. Oh . . . they say. We didn't think you wanted them . . . We're not sure where they are.

One could, of course, take a plug off something else, there being, inevitably, no spare one. One could return to the corner shop, which might still be open.

What one will in fact do is renounce the cup of tea.

Back to the sewing-machine. Find the white cotton; fit reel and spool; thread needle (the last one in the little box, incidentally). All set, at last.

Well, the machine seems to be working, anyway. Working fine, indeed. Halfway round the rim of the first mob cap in a trice. Nothing to it. Easy-peasy. This will not be too bad. Her head is perhaps throbbing a little less, too, and the limbs not fizzing quite so furiously.

And then the needle broke. A sickening little crack . . . and a stump without a point.

For a minute she sat there, simply staring. She could hear Linda calling out from the next room, asking, 'Is it nearly supper time?'

And presently the girls came to investigate the silence. They stood at the door, transfixed. And when she looked up she saw herself reflected in their eyes – their faces stiff with shock, aghast at the sight of their mother in tears, at the view of a woman they hardly recognized, weeping over a sewing-machine and a heap of white sheeting.

Season of Goodwill

The Pococks, Norma and George, drove to Birmingham three days before Christmas to do some shopping. They travelled in silence, for the most part. George was not a man given to idle chatter, and Norma was busy constructing a programme for his memorial service. George was in excellent health, and Norma a fond wife, but she was a compulsive planner. Her life was devoted to the determined marshalling of events; she was possessed by a consuming desire to impose order, to arrange, to contain, to supply a structure where structure there is none. She made lists. She devised operational strategies. She would draw up an agenda for a telephone conversation. Her time was allocated weeks in advance. The notion of the memorial service programme had been put into her head by the sight of a funeral parlour. Where others might have felt a passing chill, an intimation of mortality, Norma saw only a new area for pre-emptive arrangement. She pondered the virtues of a string trio as opposed to a pianist or someone playing, say, the oboe — George enjoyed good music. And then she noticed that the traffic was thickening, they were approaching the outskirts of the city, and she abandoned the whole exercise, which was after all a touch speculative, and turned her mind instead to her arrangements for the ensuing couple of hours. The shopping list, of course, was in her bag, and her itinerary in her head. Christmas was Norma's finest hour, the ultimate challenge. She had it licked, this year as ever. Freezer stocked, presents bought and wrapped. The current outing was a subsidiary action, a small mopping-up operation to take care of certain last-minute requirements. George, whose heart was not in it anyway, would pass the time at the library, changing books and records.

It had started to rain. Heavily. The shining black road reflected the tail-lights of cars ahead and the swags of Christmas lights adorning garages and pubs. They were navigating a big roundabout. The roadside trees were trussed with more strings of lights; neon reindeer leaped in perpetual motion ahead of a grinning Father Christmas above a car showroom. Norma liked Christmas, mainly for the opportunities it offered for triumphant management. This year they had a big family gathering on The Day, visiting in-laws tomorrow, and a sequence of commitments in the three-day run-up ahead. Of course, there were always lurking potential disruptions, those obstinate uncontrollable elements which would mar the smooth procedure of her programme – flu, snow, trouble with the cooker or the boiler, recalcitrant behaviour by relatives. But she always had contingency arrangements which could be whipped out and set in motion to cover a wide range of eventualities. She prided herself on thinking of everything. Almost everything.

Norma sat staring out of the window. She rubbed the condensation away and saw herself reflected in the glass – a small, neat woman of fifty-five with dark cropped hair and a round fresh face, which cruised now over the gleaming roads, the wind-bent trees and the occasional scurrying pedestrian. The rain was sluicing down the windscreen; the gutters ran with water. Never mind. The shopping would all be under cover; they could park in the multi-storey. She was filled with a sense of well-being, a cheery uplift of spirits. Christmas. Good.

The traffic was thick now, slowed by the rain which swept across in white sheets, blotting out visibility. George was hunched over the steering wheel, peering forward. The interior of the car was warm and intimate. Norma continued to feel expansive, and benign. Bendicks chocs, she thought, for after dinner. And something for old Mrs Freely opposite. She took out her list, and made additions.

'Awful rain . . .' she observed. 'Is your brolly in the back?'

George was mildly deaf, and did not catch this. He was also finely attuned to the tone of remarks which were inconsequential and those which were not. He grunted, merely, and continued to steer the car into the torrents. He was a big, stolid man, with an air of stoical endurance.

At this moment Norma caught sight of the boy. He was standing at the side of the road, fifty yards or so ahead, with one thumb cocked out towards the traffic – a slight, stooped, sodden figure wearing an anorak dark with water, his hair licked down to his head.

Even at the time, she could not think what had come over her.

'Pull over,' she found herself saying. 'We'll give him a lift.'

'What?' said George, startled.

'Pull in and pick that poor lad up. He's soaked through.'

As the boy opened the back door of the car and stepped in, Norma began to regret her sudden access of charitable feeling. He was going to make the upholstery all wet. And he might smoke. Oh well.

'We're going into the city centre,' she said briskly. 'That all right for you?'

The boy did not reply. He seemed to mutter something. Norma thought him either ill-mannered or overcome with diffidence. She made various remarks which, equally, met with no response and then she lapsed into silence. George said nothing. The rain continued to lash down. The car was filled now with a ripe fug – the reek of damp clothes and the pervasive presence of their passenger.

They were approaching a big intersection on the outskirts of the city. Norma addressed the boy. 'Do you want to come right into town? Or shall we put you down earlier?'

The boy spoke, at last. After twenty seconds or so. He said 'Jus' go on driving. Not into Brum. Jus' go straight on.'

Norma thought he could not have heard her properly. She said, 'We're turning off soon. Do you want to come into the centre, or shall we drop you?'

She felt the boy moving on the seat. She turned her head. And saw the boy's hand come forward, holding a gun, a small black thing which came to rest against the back of George's neck.

George said, 'Oy! What's . . .' He took one hand off the steering-wheel, as though to swot a fly.

Norma said, 'George, don't do anything. Just go on driving.' And George, perplexed, put his hand back on the wheel and tried to see what was going on in the driving mirror.

The boy had not known until then that he was going to do this. He had been going to hold up a post office, or some small shop, because someone he knew had done that and it had worked out pretty well. He had acquired the gun, and then he had set off in search of a post office or shop, but before he found one it had started chucking down and he had got fed up with the wet and decided to hitch a lift instead. And, once inside the car, he had looked at the back of the man's neck, fat and fleshy, and imagined pushing the gun into it, and remembered too that someone else he knew had held up some people in a car. So he had done it, just like that.

'George,' said Norma, 'this boy has a gun. He is pointing it at you. I think you should just go on driving while we sort things out.' She spoke very loudly and clearly; this was not an occasion for misunderstandings. She was surprised at how calm she felt. She realized that her life had spun out of control, that she was without contingency arrangements, but so far she was keeping cool. Reasonably cool.

George said, 'What does he want?'

Norma had thought, rapidly. She now spoke to the boy. 'We'll give you all the cash we have, and then put you down at the intersection. Right?' Her voice shook a bit. Maybe she wasn't quite so calm.

The boy considered this. It might do. He said, 'How much you got?'

Norma turned out her purse. She asked George for his wallet. George nodded. There was a total of thirty-five pounds and some loose change. She told the boy. This is the age of plastic money.

The boy displayed emotion for the first time. He sounded quite annoyed. 'Thass no good.'

Road signs loomed, and the swirl of the intersection.

'Take the city centre turn,' hissed Norma.

'What?' said George.

'Don't talk to each other, see?' instructed the boy. He jabbed the gun into George's neck. George flinched. 'Jus' go on driving. Straight on. Not Brum.'

They swished across the intersection, and on.

'Where, then?' said Norma. Her voice sounded shrill, even to her. Calm down. Think.

The boy had no idea what next. He had simply wanted to get out of the rain, and now he was out of it, and these people had to do what he said, which was satisfactory, but that was about as far as it went. He said, 'Shut up!'

Norma sat tense, immersed in scurrying thought. George drove. Once, he began to speak. He said, 'Look here, what

I suggest is . . .' and the boy simply said, 'Shut up!' again, and jabbed the gun.

'Listen,' said Norma. 'We'll drive to a cash dispenser, and I'll get out and get more money. Much more. Then you go, right?'

The boy could see a flaw in this, but he couldn't put a finger on it. So he said nothing. He waited – for something to happen, or for some idea to arrive.

His silence was unnerving. He breathed heavily. He had a cold, Norma realized. Automatically, she opened the window a little, while her head continued to churn. She made calculations, flew from one eventuality to another, ended up down blind alleys, retraced her steps, began again.

George drove on. The rain lashed down. The windscreen wipers whined to and fro. Norma spoke once more: 'Let us go, and you can take the car. We'll pull in, and he'll give you the keys, and you can just let us go, and take the car. Right?'

'What?' said George. 'Hang on, I'm not so sure . . .'

'No,' said the boy.

'It's J registration. GL. Automatic.'

'I can't drive, can I?' said the boy irritably.

Norma subsided, all washed up.

The boy said, 'Go to Sheffield.'

'Sheffield!' exclaimed Norma.

George said 'What?'

'He wants us to drive him to Sheffield.'

The boy had seen the name on a sign and remembered that he'd once had a mate who lived in Sheffield. He had no idea where Sheffield was. He was seventeen, and knew little.

'All right,' said Norma. She tried to catch George's eye, to tell him that she was thinking. Thinking hard. 'All right. We'll drive you to Sheffield. OK?' And in the meantime – she transmitted to George, feverishly – I'm thinking. Working something out. Just drive.

George drove. All around, Norma saw, the world was continuing on its tranquil way without them. Christmas trees twinkled in the windows of complacent homes; each shop, each filling-station, each café was jewelled with Christmas lights. It occurred to her that, if the worst came to the worst, Christmas would hurtle ahead regardless. Outrage and disbelief were added to her fear.

The boy was hungry. He'd been hungry all along, but the problem was now becoming acute. He had not eaten for quite a while, for various reasons. They passed a Happy Eater, and a McDonald's. His hunger now became his most pressing concern. He forgot about Sheffield, and tried to work out how to get food. He could take what money they'd got and tell the man to pull in, and then he'd just clear off. It wasn't raining so hard now. But they'd go to the police, and he didn't want that. Now that he'd got them, he didn't really know what to do with them. And if he didn't get some nosh soon he'd go crazy. The problem made him bad-tempered.

Within Norma's head there now boiled simultaneous sequences of thought. One of these planned, speculated, explored possibilities, telegraphed silent queries to George.

The other related what had happened – was happening – to some unspecified future listener: 'I simply don't know what came over me. We never pick up hitchhikers. But there he was, standing in the rain, and for some extraordinary reason I said to George . . .'

'Where d'you live?'

Startled, Norma told him.

'How far's that?'

She consulted George. 'Ten – twelve miles,' said George.

The boy was silent for a few moments. Then – 'Go there.'

'What's he say?' inquired George.

'He says we're to go to our house.'

Norma was now fizzing with anxiety and query. What did this mean? Suppose he . . . ? What if . . . ? She could sense George, too, ticking away beside her in calculation. He said, 'Have to turn round, you know. It's in the opposite direction.' His tone was propitiating, conciliatory. Norma took comfort from this. Take it easy, he meant. Don't annoy the fellow.

'Turn round, then,' said the boy.

George did so, at the next roundabout. They swished back across the intersection, back past the spot at which they had acquired their passenger, back past houses and shopping precincts seen earlier in what now seemed some other incarnation.

'What food you got in your house?' demanded the boy.

Norma jumped. None of them had spoken for some while.

'Food?'

Lots of food. The turkey, in the freezer. The stuffing. The pudding and the brandy butter and the smoked salmon. The *bœuf en daube* for the in-laws tomorrow evening.

Enlightenment dawned. He was hungry. Hope. Guile. 'Sausages,' she said. 'Bacon. Eggs. Baked beans.'

Or . . . A prolonged hold-up? A siege? Hope crumbled.

The boy sniffed, succulently. She wanted to hand him a Kleenex. Here he was, possibly about to shoot them, and she wanted to hand him a Kleenex. Sniffing exasperated her, always.

They were a few minutes from home now. Her thoughts ran helter-skelter, goaded by alternating hope and panic. The phone. The neighbours. Would he . . . ? Could they . . . ?

The car turned into the drive in front of the house, pulled up. George said, 'Here we are, then.' That mollifying tone, still.

The boy was agitated. It was in his voice, his movements. 'Get out and go to the door. Don't talk. Open the door and go in.'

He herded them towards the house. They both, now, saw the gun clearly – pointing at them, now at one, now at the other. It was not very big – but that didn't tell you anything, did it? Norma's experience of firearms was derived entirely from TV serials – George's also, so far as she knew. He was a personnel manager, and had got out of National Service on account of an asthmatic condition.

They were in the house. Home. But not, under these circumstances, home at all. The whole thing was unearthly

– the sort of affair you read about in newspapers, the misadventure of hapless unknown folk.

The boy was looking about him, distracted. His eye fell on the telephone. He reached out and took the receiver off. He opened the sitting-room door and looked in.

Norma sidled up to George. She muttered, 'I'm going to . . .'

The boy swung round. 'Shut up, you stupid bitch!'

It seemed to Norma that all her hair stood on end – that her neat, cropped thatch simply rose, as though electrified. She had never been addressed thus in her life. Well, not since schooldays. She felt violated. She was angry, as well as frightened.

'OK, OK,' said George. 'Let's all calm down.'

The boy could see the central problem now. It was that there were the two of them. He had remembered that the guy he'd known who'd done something like this had a mate with him. As it was, he was in difficulties. He needed the woman, to get him something to eat. The man was an encumbrance. He eyed George, thinking about this.

They stood there. The hall clock ticked – a reassuring sound, normally, which now was not. And then the boy said, 'Where's the food?'

Norma pointed to the kitchen door, speechless still.

He pushed them ahead of him again. In the kitchen, the fridge placidly hummed, the washing-machine blinked a red eye to say that its cycle was complete. The room was immaculate, the table laid ready for lunch. Christmas cards on the dresser, a scarlet poinsettia on the window ledge.

The boy looked round, and then he stared again at George in a way that neither George nor Norma cared for.

He indicated one of the chairs. 'Sit down.' He brandished the gun.

George sat.

The boy now reached for the washing-up cloths. Norma's new, matching Irish linen cloths. He fished in the pocket of his jeans and took out a knife. A small, very shiny knife. He slashed the cloths and began to rip them into strips. The Pococks watched, mesmerized: the knife, the disintegration of the cloths.

The boy tied George to the chair, making heavy weather of it. He was clumsy with his hands, Norma saw; she could have done a better job herself. The knife was tucked into his back pocket and the gun lay on the floor beside him. Norma, her head spinning, noted this – she calculated, dithered, saw George do the same – and then he was immobilized, legs strapped to the legs of the chair, arms bound together behind his back.

The boy stood up, snuffling. He wiped his nose with his hand. Then he waved towards the fridge. 'What you got in there?'

Norma walked over to the fridge and opened the door. She found the power of speech: 'Sausages . . . Bacon . . .'

The boy looked over her shoulder into the lit and furnished interior. He pointed to the *bœuf en daube*, in its casserole,

64

covered with clingfilm, waiting to be reheated for the in-laws. 'What's that?'

'It's . . . a sort of stew.'

'Take it out.'

She did so. The boy pulled off the clingfilm, sniffed. 'I'll have that. Make it hot. And some chips.'

She stared at him, aghast. It was this, perhaps, that finally broke her spirit. Sullenly, she put the casserole into the microwave.

'I've got oven chips in the freezer.'

'That'll do,' said the boy.

They watched him eat. He ate voraciously but was at last defeated by the daube, which had been intended for four. He pushed the dish to one side. He sat there for a few moments, looking thoughtful. Then he addressed George: 'Got any beer?'

George indicated the cupboard under the dresser.

Furnished with a six-pack, the boy drank a can, and then half of another. He didn't know what to do now. He found this place appallingly oppressive, and the people were getting on his nerves. He finished off the second can of beer, pondering. Then he got up and wandered around the kitchen, rummaging in drawers. He became irritable.

He turned to Norma and said, 'C'mon.'

'Now, look here . . .' George began.

'Shut up! You start anything stupid and I'll blow her head off, see?' He gave Norma a shove in the direction of the door and hustled her out into the hall. 'Upstairs!'

They climbed the stairs. Norma, seething with anxiety and indignation, saw the familiar blue pile of the carpet and then – as the boy opened doors, peered inside rooms and pushed her again ahead of him – the neat, calm and now somehow inaccessible interior of her own bedroom. She stood there, her heart thumping, while the boy looked round, and then started to fling open drawers and cupboards.

Robbery. Of course. Well, that would be a small price to pay. The insurance was all in order, naturally. Best simply to tell him where she kept her jewel-case.

'In the right-hand drawer of the dressing-table,' she said, icily.

The boy stared at her. He opened the drawer, flipped through the contents dismissively. 'Where's yer tights?'

Norma gaped.

'Tights!' said the boy furiously. 'Stupid git! I got to tie you up, haven't I?'

Her heart pounded again. The easy option of robbery evaporated.

'Get them out!' ordered the boy, and she moved stiffly to the chest of drawers in which lay new packets of tights and the plastic bags labelled LADDERED and UNLADDERED. She later realized that even in her traumatized condition her hand had fallen upon the LADDERED bag.

They went downstairs again. Norma saw at once that George had been making frantic efforts to free himself. The boy glanced suspiciously at him, thrust Norma into a chair and set about trussing her up. As a finishing touch, he now supplied each of them with a gag in the form of a pair of Norma's tights. He seemed to be in a great hurry. The job was not done with much efficiency. Norma's right foot had an inch or two of play, she found. She and George eyed each other, across the table, speculating and signalling.

The boy found some more cash in George's desk. He also found George's father's fob-watch, which he quite fancied, so he took that too. He looked at the sofa and considered having a kip, and then decided against that. He really hated this place – it gave him the creeps. So he opened the French windows and went quietly out into the garden, whence he achieved the road again by climbing over the wall. He headed at once for the sound of traffic, away from this oppressive area of silent houses and quiet streets.

As soon as he was on the busy road again, amid shops and pubs and flowing traffic, he more or less forgot the Pococks. He had a bit of money now, and he wasn't hungry any more, so what he needed was an arcade, with some really good video games. He started to look for one, and then he heard the wail of a police car, a noise he always found unsettling, so he hopped on a bus, and sat there looking out of a window until after a mile or two he spotted an arcade, and it didn't look half bad, so he hopped off again.

He left the gun in the bus, on the seat, because he had some cash now, enough to be going on with, so he didn't need it any more. The gun was found within minutes by another passenger, who happened to be a retired teacher and knew a starting pistol when he saw one and therefore was not especially perturbed, merely handing it over to the conductor for consignment to the lost property office.

It took the Pococks five minutes to be pretty certain that the boy had gone and another ten to fight their way out of their bonds. The police arrived very shortly after George's phone call; Norma heard the siren as she stood in the kitchen, her heart still banging around unnaturally, and she thought it the most exquisite sound she had ever heard. She felt as though she were surfacing from a bad dream and as she did so her normal faculties came slowly back into play. By the time the police were in the house, requiring information, she could think of nothing except how to get on course again for Christmas. She had tipped the remains of the daube into the dustbin and was busily working out a schedule for its replacement: quick foray to Sainsbury's (which would be jam-packed, dammit . . .) for the wherewithal to knock up a quick casserole for tomorrow. 'What?' she said to the policeman. 'Well, I simply don't know what came over me. But there he was, standing in the rain, and for some extraordinary reason . . .'

She felt almost steady now, but as she talked she glimpsed unnerving alternative scenarios which she did not want to contemplate, not now or ever. All that mattered was to get back to her personal struggle to harness the perverse and wilful forces all around. She did not want to think about the boy, who was even now continuing his fractured progress from one eventuality to the next, a few miles and a whole world away.

The Clarinettist and the Bride's Aunt

The best man did not dance with the bridesmaid; the bridesmaid was four and a half and the best man had other fish to fry. The bridegroom's former girlfriend cruised the reception, dressed to kill, attracting much interest and staking out territory for months to come. The bride flew hither and thither, a froth of white silk and billowing skirts, kissing and smiling. The bridegroom took his jacket off quite early on, while they were all still seated at long tables in the big gilded and beflowered ballroom of the country-house hotel. Gradually, the contained decorum induced by the church service fell away. Long before the jazz band arrived there were jackets off all around and children were scooting up and down the room, getting under the feet of the waitresses.

The wedding guests were a fine confusion of age and circumstance, the entire association of two people's lives, acquisitions by birth and by choice, gathered together thus amid the white napery and the lilies and the champagne buckets, most of them wearing unaccustomed clothes and wondering who everyone else might be. There were teachers and nurses and financial consultants and computer programmers, there were a ballet dancer and a journalist and a motor-cycle courier and a member of Parliament and a wine merchant and a hairdresser and many others. Between them, they reached away in all directions, a kaleidoscope of the time and the place from which they sprang. There were those who had scarcely begun and those who were nearly through, and those who hung out in bedsits and those whose homes would fetch half a million. They wore Austin Reed suits and Levis and leather jackets and suits from Oxfam shops, silk outfits from Jaeger and skin-tight Lycra and Monsoon dresses and two-pieces from Marks & Spencer. Each homed in upon familiar faces and eyed the rest, passing judgement. Only the bride and groom knew everyone. They presided, the stars of the event, the catalysts, the rationale for this medley which was both random and entirely ordered. This man was here because his wife was the groom's cousin, that girl was here because she had once worked with the bride. Most of them would never set eyes on one another again.

The jazz band arrived when the meal had ended, after the toasts and the speeches, when coffee was being served and people were drifting around, visiting other tables, trooping out to the cloakrooms. They arrived without fuss, were suddenly there, at one end of the room, chatting to one another and setting themselves up with a sort of unobtrusive assurance. They were a seven-piece band, all male, veering towards middle age, the trombone player and the pianist in their sixties. They filled that end of the room with the brassy shine of their instruments and their calm, purposeful presence. People did not so much notice them as become aware of them, and when they began to play it was without fuss or flourish but with the relaxed power of those who know exactly what they are about, and know also that they are doing it very well indeed. It was as though everything moved on to a different plane, as though the whole event changed gear.

They played 'Canal Street Blues' and 'Ace in the Hole' and 'Louisiana'. People got up and danced. Children bounced around on the polished floor. The wedding party proceeded beneath the level of the music in a cheerful burble and a ceaseless swirl of comings and goings. The bride's parents toured the room, paying especial attention to the old, the very young, and those who seemed to have nobody to talk to. The bridegroom's cronies hived off into a noisy group of shirt-sleeved and tieless young men and thin long-legged girls who laughed a lot. Babies wailed and were fed or swept off for a nappy-change. Those few guests who knew good jazz when they heard it gave the music three quarters of their attention and missed much of what was said to them, occasionally causing offence.

The bride's aunt, Susan Hamilton, was one of these. She had not at first noticed the arrival of the band, busy exchanging polite nothings with a relative, but when they began to play she felt at once a thrill of appreciation. Oh yes, she thought, oh yes. She disengaged herself tactfully from the relative and moved to a seat where she could see the band more clearly. She noted that unforced power, the fluency of people who are on top of the job. This was the real thing all right. The trombone player was amazing. They were into 'Snake Rag' now. Very nice too. The clarinettist took a solo.

And as he did so she saw who he was. This man, ten feet away from her, playing the clarinet like nobody's business, was the one-time love of her life, the first and only. James Carlisle. Him.

Older. Of course. Thicker. Slight stoop. Wearing white shirt, dark trousers, red-striped waistcoat, and still playing jazz clarinet fit to break your heart. Just like back then in smoky cellars choked with students and awash with rot-gut cheap wine. Better, indeed. He'd been good, back then. He was stunning, now.

Well, she thought. Well. She gazed. She felt the incredulous smile that spread across her face.

Halfway through the solo he saw her. He looked directly at her and continued to do so. His playing did not change, his expression did not flicker, but he played now, she became complacently aware, directly to her. For her. He played and she listened and they looked at one another, for what seemed a very long time.

The number came to an end. The leader of the band announced that they would now take a short break. And the clarinettist, still looking directly at the bride's aunt, cocked his thumb in the direction of the double doors that opened into the gardens.

They met at the top of the flight of steps leading down

on to an acreage of brilliant lawn. 'Breath of fresh air, I thought . . .' said James Carlisle.

They proceeded down the steps and arrived at a bench overlooking the grass. They sat down, and set about a mutual examination. The years did not fall away — oh no. Rather, they gathered around them in an interesting haze, a mysterious screen of untransmittable experience. Here we are, each thought, the same and not at all the same.

'I won't say I'd have known you anywhere,' he observed. 'It was the way you had your head on one side. You always did that in the Union cellars. Head on one side. Slightly critical expression.'

'I didn't spot you at once. Only when you started playing. In the street, we'd have walked past each other, I imagine.'

'Well, what luck,' he said.

'I take it this isn't what you do? I mean, day in day out . . .'

'Would that it were. I'm a statistician by trade. This is a spot of moonlighting. Ditto for most of us. Our trombone player is an antiquarian bookseller. And what brings you here?'

'I am the bride's aunt.'

James Carlisle laughed.

'And why is that funny?' she inquired.

'Just that I would never have thought of you as being anyone's aunt. But I can quite see how these things happen.'

'Oh, they do indeed. Before you know where you are.'

'Nice girl, is she?'

'Delightful. My favourite niece. I have three.'

At the far side of the sweep of grass a bride was posing for a photograph, a swirl of white against the green.

'More photos?' said Susan. 'I thought they'd done all that.'

'This is not your bride. Different outfit, if you look. There's another wedding going on in the annexe over there. It's absolutely the thing these days – marriage. We're booked up for weeks to come. Not that we take just anything, I'll have you know. We pick and choose a bit.'

'How did Natalie and David get to hear about you?'

'Let's see now . . . Oh yes – the bridegroom knew a bloke whose girlfriend had been at a wedding we did and got chatting to someone in the band.'

'And so here we are today . . .'

'So here we are today. Quirk of fate.'

'Do you ever see any of that crowd?' she asked. 'From back then.'

'I do not. You?'

'Nobody. One loses touch, somehow.'

Each considered, for an instant, the impenetrable mass of the intervening years, and decided to let them be.

'I like your dress,' said James.

'Thank you.'

'I've become a connoisseur of wedding outfits. You see some pretty odd gear, I can tell you.'

'How many do you chalk up, then? Weddings.'

'This time of year – height of the season – you can reckon on one a week.'

'Gracious . . .' she said.

'And do they know what they're at, one asks?'

She shot him a look. Something glimmered, it would seem, from that impenetrable mass.

'Let no man put asunder . . .' he continued. 'Well, there'll be a fair amount of putting asunder, I don't doubt. Nothing personal, of course – I daresay your nice niece is all set for eternal bliss. Just statistics, that's all.'

'Statistics . . .' she said. 'Of course, when it's going on, you never feel quite like a statistic.'

He, now, shot a glance.

'Married yourself, are you?' he inquired, after a moment.

'Not now. Up till three years ago I was.'

'Me too. Not – I mean.'

There was a silence. They gazed reflectively at the photographic session in the distance. The bride and groom, flanked now by the complementary pairings of their parents.

'How about I take our glasses in for a top-up?' said James Carlisle.

'Have we time?'

'Plenty of time.'

She watched him go up the steps, holding the empty champagne glasses. The same, and not at all the same. Well, well. Just fancy.

There came to her, now, various images from back then, frozen like clips from a film, images which presumably he shared and upon which it seemed wiser not to dwell. She fended these off, observed the distant group (now marshalling recalcitrant bridesmaids) and thought about pairings.

Back in the days of the Jazz Club and the Union Cellars there had been pairings – definitely there had been pairings. But it had been tacitly understood that these were transitory, temporary, that they were for the term, or for a week or two, or just for the evening. And, likewise, there were those who were couples, and were known and recognized as such, but it was known and recognized equally that couplings could become uncoupled, with the greatest of ease and quite possibly with no hard feelings.

'Goodness . . .' she thought, knowing what she now knew. How was it done? What innocence. What primal innocence.

The pairings, back then, had been pairings of mutual convenience and intellectual pairings and sporting pairings and pairings of undisguised carnality. From time to time a girl got pregnant and vanished from the scene, amid commiserations. Very rarely, a couple got married, prompting shock and unconcealed disapproval. They then went to live in squalor in a bedsit or flat and nobody visited them. Marriage was not at all the thing, back then. Definitely not.

Except that, eventually, after a few years, many of them got married. Not to one another but to completely different people encountered in the real world of job applications and mortgages. Others, of course, did not, for various reasons.

James Carlisle returned, with glasses of champagne. He had fended off his colleagues, been introduced to bride and groom and shaken the hand of the bride's mother. The bride's mother was a little distracted at that moment, looking round for her sister, whom she did not seem to have seen for some while. She hoped Susan hadn't got stuck with someone tiresome.

He sat down again. 'Marriage,' he said, 'is an act of such extraordinary optimism.'

'Too right.'

'The young, of course, tend to be optimistic. And so they damn well should.'

'Were we? I can't remember.'

'It's not something one remembers – a state of mind. It's precise things you remember.'

'True,' she said. She carefully did not look at him, now, but gazed out over the grass. The photo session was over; the bridesmaids were whooping it up like foals, to the detriment of their dresses.

'Hm . . .' He had decided, evidently, to drop that. 'Yes, well . . . Actually, I'm deficient in that area, myself. Tell me something – I didn't ever propose marriage, did I? Back then.'

'Good heavens, no,' she said.

'You'd have slapped me in the face, no doubt.'

'Well . . . It would have seemed a distinct breach of manners, I think.'

'I'm glad I behaved myself, then.'

'Oh . . .' she said. 'You were splendid, always.'

'You were pretty good yourself,' said James Carlisle.

They looked at each other, now, and hugely grinned.

'Dear me,' said Susan Hamilton. 'This won't do at all. Surely you should be getting back to your duties?'

'All in good time.'

'And I have not yet done my stuff with the in-laws. Nor with Natalie's boss nor my sister's best friend. What are you going to play, after the interval?'

'What would you like us to play?'

'It's hardly up to me.'

'If that's how you feel I'll have to trust to my memory. I think I still know your tastes.'

And so, in due course, they left their bench, and the fresh air, and returned to the wedding. The band struck up. Couples took to the floor. The bride danced with her father. The bride's mother, anxiously inspecting the room, caught sight of her sister once more, sitting a little apart, being talked at by the groom's parents, and thought that Susan was looking extremely ... vibrant. She knew that look, but could not quite put a finger on it.

The wedding continued. The cake was cut. The best man achieved a couple of objectives. The groom's former girlfriend consolidated ground. The bridesmaid began to flag, tearfully, and was removed. The older guests drifted to the perimeter of the room and became spectators. The band played on; the dancing became more energetic; outside the windows, twilight gathered. And all the while, above and beyond the music, isolated amid the chatter and the comings and the goings, the clarinettist and the bride's aunt watched each other – thoughtful, speculative and alert.

Marriage Lines

The Dawsons, who were having their marriage counselled, glared at each other across their counsellor. The counsellor, known to them as Liz, was a small plump woman who might have been thought attractive had any concessions been made by way of becoming clothes or a flattering haircut. As it was, her manner and appearance spoke of responsibilities heavily borne and an implacable confidence in her own judgement. She treated the Dawsons with maddening patience and impartiality, as though they were children in a nursery school whose behaviour was wayward but inevitable. Her bland attention to their complaints implied that she had heard it all before, that they were in no way unique or especially blighted, and that nothing could jolt her from her complacent consideration of their various sources of discord. She drove Ben Dawson to a frenzy. Sometimes the ferocity of his feelings about Liz quite distracted him from his irritation with his wife and the matter in hand.

'And another thing,' Prue Dawson was saying, 'I thought it was settled that when we disagree about how to handle a situation over the children we don't give conflicting instructions but we sit down and talk it over. And now only yesterday you walk in and completely undermine what I've already sorted out. That business with Nicky about the ballet shoes and next Tuesday.'

Liz turned to Ben. 'Do you have a problem with that, Ben?'

This was Liz's favourite question. Or comment, or way of moving on, or whatever it was. So far it had been clocked up five times in this session.

'Yes,' he said sourly. 'Or it wouldn't have been mentioned, would it?'

'Would you like to tell us about this, Ben?' Liz continued.

'No, to be honest. For two reasons – I should find it unspeakably boring, and Prue would get more annoyed than she is already. I daresay you might get something out of it, but I'm not sure what.'

Liz fixed him with her most neutral gaze. 'Thank you for sharing that with us, Ben.'

It occurred to Ben, not for the first time, that he might simply walk out. The only thing that stopped him was that such a move would undoubtedly be interpreted to his disadvantage and held against him. Principally by Liz.

He stared at the floor, which was the only place to look if you were not to catch someone else's eye. The chairs were arranged in a semicircle, so that Liz sat between her clients. They were chairs of an awkward lowness, forcing the occupant to sit with legs stuck out straight ahead, in a parody of relaxation. The only window was covered by a blind, to exclude reminders of ordinary life in the world beyond. The room was profoundly claustrophobic, which was presumably the intention. Concentrate, it said. Bare your soul. Expose yourself. Go on – wallow in it.

He said, 'Do you mind if we talk about something else now?'

Liz gave Prue the glance of measured impartiality. 'How do you feel about that, Prue?'

'I don't care one way or the other,' said Prue. 'Incidentally,' she added, speaking across Liz to Ben, 'in the end it turned out the wretched ballet shoes were the wrong size. I'll have to get another pair. God knows how, before Tuesday.'

'Are you married, Liz?' said Ben, after a moment. 'Or have you been?'

Liz dealt him a chilly smile. 'That's irrelevant, Ben, isn't it?'

'No, I don't think it is, really. It's a question of credentials. I mean, to advise us you have to have some experience of our situation, don't you?'

'Let's just say I'm in a relationship,' said Liz. The tone of stern professional neutrality once more.

If I hear that dire word again I'll scream, thought Ben. 'Good,' he said. 'Join the club.' He looked at Prue. 'I daresay I could take her to get some shoes tomorrow. I could leave the office early.'

'Oh, right,' said Prue. 'Thanks.'

Liz cleared her throat. She shuffled the papers on her lap. These actions, the Dawsons now knew, meant that she felt the focus of attention had strayed and that she needed to establish control. 'I've noticed that you both mention work quite a bit today. Maybe that's an area we should cover. Ben, could I ask you what you feel about Prue's work situation?'

'What do you mean – what do I *feel* about it? Are you asking if I think she's got a good job, or a suitable job, or are you asking if I think she ought to be working in WC1 rather than WC2, or what, for heaven's sake?'

Liz reflected, eyeing him. At last she said, 'It's interesting that you seem to be getting a bit overexcited, Ben. Do you want to say anything about this?'

'Only that I wish you'd use language with rather more precision.'

Liz turned to Prue. 'What do you feel about Ben's attitude here?'

'Actually I think he's got a point,' said Prue.

Ben shot his wife a look of surprise.

'You think he has a problem with your work situation?' said Liz encouragingly.

'No, I mean I think he's right about language. Sometimes we all have a problem over what it is exactly we're trying to talk about.'

Ben experienced a gust of something suspiciously like affection. 'In point of fact,' he said, 'work is not a prime area of dissension. I entirely approve of Prue's job. I think she's good at it. I try to be supportive.'

'Hm . . .' said Prue.

'Well, all right. I agree I was a touch unreasonable about

the Leeds trip. Next time I'll shut up. But . . .' – he addressed himself to Liz – '. . . by and large and on the whole work is not something we have rows about. I appreciate that Prue's work is important to her, and that she does it well. I don't resent that. I don't suspect her of sleeping with her colleagues, either.'

Liz's expression of shrewd appraisal meant, he now recognized, that he had said something of deep significance. 'I wonder why you said that, Ben?'

'It was a joke. A rather stupid joke. I was trying to lighten things up a bit.'

'But you said it. There's some sort of sexual tension there, then?'

'Oh, Christ . . .' said Ben wearily.

Prue said, 'Actually there isn't. That's something else we're not in fact quarrelling about. We don't suspect each other of having it off with someone else.'

Liz faintly smiled. She shook her head slightly. 'In fact, Prue, I'm going to suggest that next time you have a full psychosexual session. Doctor Chambers handles that.'

'I thought you were our counsellor?' said Prue.

'Not for psychosexual. That's a separate area.'

'I'm surprised,' said Ben. 'This is interesting. You're suggesting then that the sexual element of marriage is a thing apart? I'd have thought that was a trifle unorthodox.'

'I'm not trained for psychosexual, that's all.'

'You specialize in straight domestic wrangling and child-rearing disputes, is that right?'

There was a silence. Liz now wore her expression of personal distaste modulated by infinite professional patience. 'Ben, I'm going to have to say that I think you have a serious attitude problem. This is not something to make jokes about.'

'That wasn't a joke,' said Ben. 'It was a conversational style. And I was asking a question.'

Liz turned to Prue. 'Do you have a problem with the way Ben talks, Prue?'

'No,' said Prue. 'Not particularly.' There was a distinct edge of irritation to her voice. 'Possibly it takes a bit of getting used to.'

Liz frowned slightly. 'Has this adjustment been difficult for you?'

'*No*,' said Prue. She glanced rather wildly at Ben, who grimaced. Prue looked at him again and then away, quickly. 'No, that's not the point. Actually it's one of the things I like about Ben.'

'I see.' Liz was now registering muted disapproval.

'There are quite a lot of things I like about Ben,' Prue went on determinedly. 'And in fact I think there are things he likes about me.'

Liz sighed. 'Prue, we're getting off course again, aren't we?'

'Well, I must say I don't quite see . . .' Prue began.

'Compatibility is irrelevant, is it?' said Ben.

Liz turned to him. She was impregnable, he saw. He read in her face absolute complacency and an unswerving rectitude. 'Ben,' she was saying, 'I think we're in trouble again with your basic attitude. I feel that . . .' Language oozed from her, smothering him.

It came to him with sudden clarity that there was something dreadfully awry. He could not imagine how they had arrived in this room, locked into eerie collaboration with this dispiriting woman. He recognized with elation that Prue's discomfort matched his own feverish impatience. He got to his feet. He said, 'Liz, thank you for trying to help us, but speaking for myself I feel there's nothing further I can contribute. I don't know about Prue, but . . .'

Prue also had risen. 'Yes,' she said. 'Me too, in fact. Thank you very much, Liz, but . . .'

They fled. They stepped into the street, still trailing their unfinished excuses. They headed for home, side by side, bolstered by the familiar private apposition of disagreement and collusion which seemed now a protection rather than a constraint.

The Cats' Meat Man

She opened the front door and there he was on the step, wearing a white coat. Like someone behind the deli counter in Tesco, she told her daughter later. Not as clean as it might have been, either – the coat.

'Yes?' she said.

'Do you like good food?' he gabbled. 'Interested in good food, are you?' She saw the van now, parked in her little bit of driveway. A small blue van. 'Chicken Kiev. Lasagne. Prawns. Dover sole.' He had a white pasty face in which his sloe dark eyes darted about like fish in a tank – looking here, there, everywhere except at her. 'Beef Stroganoff?' he urged. 'Fond of Beef Stroganoff at all?'

'No,' she said. 'Not really. I eat vegetables mostly. And egg dishes. Eggs Florentine. Do you know that? With spinach.'

Freeze-dried, he told her. It's the new process. Not just frozen – air-dried. Or air-blown, did he say, or airbrushed. Something like that. Anyway, not just straightforward frozen, she explained to her daughter. More up to date than that.

It was six o'clock. Probably he hadn't made a sale all afternoon, she thought. Dead on his feet now, and still having to burble on about air-dried and Beef Whatsit. The people at the farmhouse wouldn't have taken anything, that was for sure, and the Holly Cottage family were away on their holidays and old Mrs Hammond wouldn't have so much as answered the door.

'Do you know what you've reminded me of?' she said. 'The cats' meat man. When I was a child. He'd come down the street with his handcart, ringing a bell. And you'd see all the cats come out, all along the row, and hang around. He'd have this great big wet red slab and he'd cut off a slice for you. Sixpence. And lights, he'd have. I'm not sure what bit of an animal that is. Have you any idea?'

The man looked in her direction. His eyes continued to twitch this way and that. 'I couldn't say. We don't do any of those. Just prime T-bone steak. £4.50 each. Beautiful quality.'

'I haven't got £4.50 to spare, I'm afraid. That's as much as I spend on food in two or three days.'

He was opening up the back of the van now. 'Individually packaged,' he was saying. 'All ready to store in your freezer.' She saw tier upon tier of metal trays in which were stacked flat cardboard boxes. He took one out and opened it up: she saw neat overlapping fillets of fish. 'Lemon sole. £6.50.'

'Too much,' she said firmly. 'I suppose I could run to a few fish fingers.'

'We don't do those.' He sounded sulky now. That'll get you nowhere, she thought. Smile and smile, if you're a salesman – that's the trick. But he was wiped out, you could see that. He swayed as he stood there waving his packets of this and that.

'It was the same cats' meat man right up till I was fifteen,' she said. 'We never knew his name. We went through several cats, they'd come to grief one way or another, but always the same cats' meat man. Big fellow that could cut up meat like nobody's business.'

He stared at her. No, not stared – looked her way and his eyes went on flickering around. Not a straightforward sort of a man, she rather thought.

'Oh, all right,' she said. 'I'll have one of those Chicken Kiev things. Just the one portion. I'll get my purse.' She paused. He looked as though he was in a daze now. Oh, for heaven's sake, she thought, show a bit of Christian charity, Eileen. 'If you like to come in for a minute, I've got a pot of tea made. You look as though you could do with a cup.'

He muttered. Wouldn't mind . . . or something like that. Not – That's very kind of you. Oh, well.

He trailed after her into the house. She put him in the basket chair in the kitchen. The tea had gone cold. 'I'll make a fresh pot,' she said. 'This is no good to man nor beast. Won't take a minute. This'll be your last call today anyway, I should think.'

He muttered again.

She filled the kettle, rinsed out the pot. 'My father did house to house for a bit,' she said. 'Selling vacuum cleaners. This was before the war. He was a warehouse clerk really, but he lost his job and then you had to take what you could. I suppose it's like that again now.' There wasn't much milk in the jug so she went through into the larder to get some more from the fridge. 'And then the war came,' she said. 'And solved that problem at least. Plenty of jobs for everyone then. Not that I'd suggest that again as a solution.' She looked across at him and he'd fallen asleep, if you please. Fast asleep in her chair with his head poked forward on his chest and that grubby white coat open to show a T-shirt with a Mickey Mouse on it. Scruffy sports shoes on his feet. My father wore a suit, she told him. Suit and tie and a clean shirt every day. And his shoes polished so you could see your face.

She poured herself a cup of tea and drank it reading the local paper. The free one that came through the door. The paper seemed to be mostly about food too. Pizzas brought to your door and Indian takeaways and three-course family lunch at the Red Lion for £5.99. She read all about this, and skimmed the Used Car column and had a look at the Property Section and still the man slept. She drank a second cup of tea, glancing at him occasionally. This is all very well, she thought. Another five minutes and I'll wake him. His mouth was open now, not a pretty sight.

She needed to go to the loo, so she got up and went upstairs. She took her time and made a bit of a noise up there, on purpose, running taps and so forth. That would get him moving, with any luck.

She came down and he wasn't there. She looked at her

bag, on the dresser, and saw that neither was her purse. And she noticed at once that the small jug was gone off the dresser and the carriage clock from the mantelpiece. She stood for a moment and her daughter hovered in the air in front of her, mouthing things. Were you completely out of your mind, Mum? Letting a perfect stranger into the house. *Asking* him in.

Oh, be quiet, you, she said. All right, all right.

She went outside, round the corner into the driveway and the van was still there. He was sitting in the driving seat, fiddling with something. She saw at once what had happened.

She walked up and looked at him through the open window. Whiter than before he was, if possible, pasty white and his eyes flickering as he kept turning the key in the ignition. Click, whirr. Click, whirr.

'Oh dear,' she said. 'What a nuisance for you.'

He muttered. Swearing. She could see that from his face, though she couldn't catch the words. Click, whirr. Click, whirr.

She watched, interested. 'Oh dear,' she said again.

Click, whirr. His eyes swivelled in her direction, then away, then back. Frantic, he was.

'Better come back in,' she said. 'Then we can ring the garage at the crossroads. They'll come out and have a look at it, I daresay.'

He swore again. Got out of the van, opened up the bonnet and stared into the van's innards. Poked at a wire. Took out a plug and put it back again. He didn't know t'other from which, you could see that.

'Suit yourself,' she said. 'But you can use the phone if you want to.'

He straightened up and eyed her. Not knowing how to take it. Wondering. *Mum!* shrieked her daughter. Oh, be quiet, she said. I wasn't born yesterday. Watch this.

He said something about a spanner.

'I'd have thought you'd have a toolkit with you,' she said sternly. 'Come back in then and I'll have a look.'

He followed her inside. 'I'll have to go upstairs,' she said. 'That sort of thing's in the landing cupboard. You may as well have that cup of tea now. Sit down.'

He looked relieved. He thought she hadn't noticed. The purse, the jug, the clock. She put the kettle on and went upstairs. When she came down with the spanner he was in the chair again. She made the tea and poured him a cup. This time he said thank you. She sat down herself, and watched him. Sweating, he was. She could see his skin glistening. She'd seldom come across such an unhealthy look. Her mother always used to say you can tell at a glance if a person's constipated. She knew now what was meant. All that expensive food in the back of the van and there he was looking like death warmed up.

'Fish is all very fine, I suppose,' she said, 'but too much red meat never did anyone any good. All that steak you've got out there. Fresh fruit and vegetables – that's what I go for myself.'

'It's nothing to do with me, is it?' he said. 'It's the firm's, not mine. Nothing to do with me what lines they decide to put out. Sell it on commission, that's all I do.'

'You don't reckon that much with the Beef Whatsit, then?'

'I didn't say that.' He was cross with himself now, knew he'd overstepped the mark. 'It's all good stuff.'

She studied him. 'Been doing this long?'

He shook his head. He didn't want to talk, but he was trapped. By the tea, the spanner, by what he thought she didn't know. 'I had a fast-food business. I used to do the lay-bys. Buffalo Bill's Pull-In – hamburgers and that. Had to pack it in.'

'What a pity,' she said. 'Why?'

She understood him to say something about a problem with his accountants. He got out a filthy bit of Kleenex and wiped his face. Pouring sweat he was, and she wouldn't have called the room hot – just nicely warm. She watched him thoughtfully. He was breathing in a funny way, too.

'One thing I should tell you,' she said. 'It's not silver, that jug. It's Britannia metal. I doubt if it's worth much. More tea?'

He twitched violently. His eyes went mad. She wondered if he'd make a run for it. *And then I'll be left with a van full of steak and prawns. Air-dried or whatever it is. Either that or he's a different type altogether and he'll get out a knife and go for me.*

She felt a bit queasy, thinking that. Somewhere, her daughter was wailing *I told you so.*

He put the teacup down with a crash. But he didn't get up. He sat there making a sort of panting noise. He was green now, rather than white, like mouldy bread.

'You know,' she said, 'I don't think you're feeling very well today, are you?'

He stared at her. 'Be all right in a minute,' he said thickly. He swayed.

'Well, it's your choice, but if I was you I'd cut my losses and get on the phone to that garage.' She thought she'd put that rather well. He could work out for himself what was meant by losses. Not that he looked as though he was up to working anything out just at that moment. No knife, she decided, he's not the type. Thanks be. So you can stop squawking, she told her daughter.

He clutched his throat and made a sort of gargling noise. And then he keeled over. He slumped forward and if she hadn't come across and propped him up he'd have toppled forward on to the floor. His eyes rolled up till she could see only the whites and for a moment she thought he'd died until she realized she could still hear him breathing, in that gasping way. She considered him. If a person's fainted you put their head between their knees, but she didn't somehow feel that was the problem here. She wondered if she was seeing a heart attack. But he wasn't more than thirty or so, by her reckoning. It's the likes of me who have heart attacks, she thought, not someone his age.

She waited a couple of minutes and when he showed no sign of rallying she picked up the phone.

She didn't go out to the van until the ambulance had come and gone, and him with it, strapped to a stretcher in a red blanket. The ambulance men had been noncommittal, and had become even more so when they discovered the patient was neither here nor there to her, as it were. At first they'd assumed he was her son, until she'd put them right, rather sharply. After that it was just a matter of bundling him off and she'd never know, she realized, if it was heart or terminal indigestion or what.

She found her purse and the jug and the clock under the passenger seat of the van, wrapped in a couple of sheets of the *Sun*. She also found the address and phone number of the food company on an invoice pad under the dashboard and left a message on their answering machine to tell them where their van was and to request them to remove it first thing tomorrow morning.

She then returned to the van and opened up the back. She pulled out the metal trays, one by one. She took several packs of Chicken Kiev, some Dover sole and something called Vegetarian Lasagne, which might suit her. Think of it as a parking charge, she told the food company. Then, as an afterthought, she took four portions of Beef Stroganoff. Her daughter and the daughter's boyfriend, who were coming to lunch on Sunday, wouldn't know what had hit them.

A Christmas Card to One and All

Happy Christmas!

Well, here I am again, your faithful friend (sister, cousin, aunt, etc.). I can hear you thinking – My goodness! Here's Lizzie's round robin, it must be December already. Too right, doesn't time fly and here we are at number twenty-seven with another year gone by and lots to tell as usual.

Where shall I begin, my dears? I know you're dying to hear about Jenny's wedding, but all in good time, first things first. Everyone's alive and kicking and yours truly if I may say so is looking pretty snappy these days with a snazzy new hairdo (auburn highlights and a little fringe) *and* I've lost five pounds which I reckoned justifies some new glad rags for the festive season (red velveteen with a low scoop neckline – whoops!). And if any of you out there are thinking mutton dressed as lamb, kindly refrain. Actually it's my dear old Ron who could do with some sprucing up – of course he is ten years older than I am but the hairline's receding so fast it's practically out of sight and as for the waistline, well, we won't go into that. The exercise bike I got him last year (remember?) wasn't a huge success though if you ask me those pains were indigestion pure and simple, our doctor's always been a scaremonger and Ron's heart's as sound as a bell. I get him out jogging every morning and that should help the waist but it's not going to grow the hair, is it? Never mind, I'm working on that – just leave it to Lizzie.

Of course saying goodbye to the firm after thirty years was a bit of a jolt, but retirement's the best time of your life they say and I'll be seeing to it that he doesn't just sit back and atrophy. We'll start off as we mean to go on, I said to myself, so the very first morning he came down to find this super wall chart up in the kitchen – Ron's Year Plan – all done out pretty with different coloured felt pens by his loving wife. Week One – Re-decorate Spare Bedroom. Then, Turn Out Garage, Fix Guttering, Re-lay Garden Path. And so on. With some fun things thrown in too, of course – Creative Writing classes at the Poly and Car Maintenance and Upholstery at the Evening Institute. It's been going pretty well though I will say he flags a bit from time to time and I have to get in there and give him a kindly prod. Dear old Ron – where would he be without Lizzie? you're saying to yourselves. Oh well, you know me – backbone of the family. Of course there've been one or two set-backs with the scheme. He must have been careless with that ladder – the guttering isn't *that* high – but luckily it was only a simple fracture and the arm's just fine now, or all but. Equally he didn't *have* to drop a slab of paving on his toe, did he? Silly old butter-fingers.

Anyway, that's enough of Ron – it's time I got on to

everyone else. It's lovely having Kate and her Sam and the children just a few streets away. Thank heaven they *are* because I can be in and out to lend Kate a hand whenever I've got a moment. And, frankly, to keep an eye on things. I mean, if there's one thing I do know about it's bringing up children. I didn't have four of my own for nothing. Not to speak of running a house – I mean that's what I'm all about and I think I've made a pretty good job of it. I know it's unfashionable these days but I've always believed in putting family first and I'm proud of it! So there! Good for Lizzie! I can hear you saying. Anyway . . . obviously I'm only too happy to show Kate what's what and take some of the load off her when I can. Of course, her ways aren't my ways entirely – in fact if you ask me that house is a bit of a mess (ssh!), but at least I've been able to make an impact here and there. They were away for the weekend last month so I slipped round while they were gone and gave the whole place a good scrub and clear out. I really went to town, I can tell you – I was ever so pleased with myself. I switched the sitting-room furniture round while I was about it, for a surprise – I've always thought they had that sofa in the wrong place. And I went through the wardrobe and sorted out all the things that were fit only for Oxfam (Kate and I never have seen eye to eye about clothes) and I had a good go at the garden. Of course, I hadn't realized Sam wanted all those old computer magazines or I wouldn't have thrown them out, and frankly to my mind all that stuff I pulled up was weed, but gardening's never been my strong point, that

I will admit. But as I say, it's wonderful having them near enough to be able to pop in and out and help. Actually Kate says they're thinking of moving, which seems barmy to me. People don't know when they're well off.

And now I'll get to the wedding – that's what you're waiting for, I know. Jenny's. Jenny is the pretty one, by the way, for any of you we've got a bit out of touch with. Kate's the homey one and Jenny's the pretty one and Sue's the clever one and Peter's thank God we've managed a boy at last! That's what I used to tell everyone, when they were younger. Well, we had it at the White Hart Hotel, sit-down lunch for seventy. Champagne of course and a three-tier cake and a lovely man I heard about who does an old-time music medley on the piano. Actually we had quite a tussle with Jenny and Tom about it before. It seemed what they'd had in mind was some sort of informal do with a disco, if you please. I said – look, Dad and I haven't been saving up for this for nothing, we're going to do things nicely and I don't want to hear another word. It's the first family wedding, after all. I mean, Kate slipped off to a registry office like that without telling a soul, heaven knows why. I was a bit miffed at the time, quite honestly. I mean – what's a mother *for* if not to fix up a wedding? Organizing is my *forte*, though I sez it myself. Just leave it to me, I said to Jenny. Sit back and enjoy. Poor darling, she was in such a stew, the weeks before – you'd have thought she hadn't got any faith in her mum!

She looked lovely, of course. She made the dress herself – ivory satin, very simple. That's her style, I suppose. Bit *too* simple, in my view, so I laid on this little surprise – I had this lovely corsage made up of silk roses in a gorgeous deep magenta, with a little coronet to match, and I whipped it out just as she'd finished dressing. You should have seen her face! She was quite overcome – I thought she was going to burst into tears! 'My treat, darling,' I said, and I pinned them on myself. It made all the difference.

My other surprise came after lunch. I'd insisted on speeches, of course – though they started off being silly about that too, said they'd rather not have any. So I had to insist, and anyway I already had my little joke in mind. Trust Lizzie! you're thinking – always the life and soul of the party! Obviously speech-making isn't Ron's thing, and I knew he was dreading it, so when the moment came I popped up and I said, 'Hello, everyone! This is my blow for women – you're getting a mother-of-the-bride speech today for a change.' I'd got it all worked out though I hardly needed my notes when it came to the point, after all the one thing a mother remembers is what her children did. That was it, you see. I told all sorts of lovely stories about Jenny – from when she was small right till now. I daresay I may have gone on rather, but I wanted to make sure I got all the best bits in. Like the time she wet her knickers at her first pantomime and the time she came last in the obstacle race at the school sports and got stuck in the drainpipe. Of course she's slimmed down a lot since then – I'm sure they were absolutely amazed to hear she was called Fatso at school. Oh, and then I had to give a run-down on her past boyfriends – I knew Tom wouldn't mind – and of course I made it really amusing, putting the pros and cons for each of them and giving them all a star rating. Actually I forgot until I was in the middle of it that a couple of them were among the guests but I'm sure they took it in the right spirit. Anyway, it went down a treat, I can tell you – there wasn't a sound for a moment after I'd sat down and Jenny bless her was almost reduced to tears again, I could see.

Tom's really nice and just right for her but he's quite a shy chap – needs bringing out a bit, to my mind. So . . . hang on to your seats, this is really going to slay you . . . so my next bright idea was the little joke I fixed up for their first night at the honeymoon hotel – some little place in the Lake District, actually I thought it sounded a bit tame but Tom likes hiking and he'd been there before. Anyway, I arranged for one of those Kissogram girls to turn up in the middle of dinner – you know, just in bra and pants and sequins, really funny – and sing 'Love is the Sweetest Thing' to them, with love from Mum and Dad. Actually I was afraid the girl hadn't turned up because Jenny never said anything at all about it so I had to ask in the end, but apparently she had, so that was all right.

It's time I got on to the rest of the family. Well, Sue did get into college! Miss Education, I call her now. She's sharing a place with some other students and when I ring up I say, 'Can I speak to my little Miss Education, please!' Mind, it was a near thing – her A-level results weren't quite as good as she'd hoped so I thought, here we go, this is where I come in. I mean, these people can't know what someone's really like just from exam results, can they? Only a person who's close knows that. So I got on the phone and rang round the authorities in the colleges she was applying to and gave them each a good long spiel about how she'd have done better if she hadn't had that spat with the boy she's been going out with and how she's always had a tricky time with her periods and in my opinion she got a bad start at that first school when Ron was with the firm in Sevenoaks. None of them said much, the authorities I talked to, but I should imagine they must have been grateful – I mean, what a job, having to pick and choose among all those schoolchildren, obviously they need all the help they can get. Anyway, it must have done the trick because she got her college place, though between you and me I'd have liked to see a spot more gratitude for my efforts from our Sue. But I didn't say anything. They'll thank me in the long run, I say to myself, even if they can't bring themselves to do so at the time.

Which brings me to Peter. He's fifteen now, believe it or not. I still think of him as the baby. We've had our ups and downs, this year, with Peter – but you expect the odd problem with teenagers, don't you, and if I've not had experience I don't know who has. What I think is, you should jolly them through it – make a joke of the trials and tribulations. Peter's got appalling acne, of course, so I say to him every morning – 'Come on, now, let's count the spots! Whoops! There's a new one in the bottom-left-hand corner today!' Of course, not everyone can deal with it like that but I think I've got a knack with the light touch. He's always had a bit of trouble with his stammer, our Peter, so I try to turn that into a laugh as well – P-p-p-Peter, I call him. We have to make do with what we are, in this world, I tell him. All right, so you're not Rupert Everett, I tell him, but so what? Looks aren't everything. Sooner or later we're going to find out where your talents lie and then the sky's the limit!

So that's the family. And what's Lizzie been up to on her own account? you're wondering. How has Lizzie improved the shining hour? Well, I haven't let the grass grow, I promise you. Yours truly is well to the fore in the local branch of Age Concern, ferrying my little group around once a week, and a good time is had by one and all. Bar the odd mishap, of course, like the occasion I left two old dears behind on Brighton Pier, but they got themselves back in the end and a bit of an adventure is just what you need at that age. And then there's the Keep Fit class – we have it here every Tuesday afternoon – with only Ron and Peter around now there's plenty of room so I clear out the sitting-room and we have a fine old time in our leotards. We have the church Bring and Buys here now too, and the Residents' Association committee and the Animal Welfare Group meetings and the Readers' and Writers' Club.

Ron joins me in saying Hello! God bless! to all of you. He's gone out fishing for the day. Fishing's something he's taken up lately, funny old thing – I wouldn't have thought it was his cup of tea, really, sitting on the edge of a reservoir in the rain. I mean, he likes his creature comforts, does our Ron. Anyone would think he wanted to get out of the house!

So – here's Lizzie signing off at the end of another year of happy family life here at number twenty-seven, and wishing all of you the same for the year ahead.

The Five Thousand and One Nights

You may well have wondered about the subsequent marital history of Scheherazade and the Sultan. Did they live happily ever after? Well, of course not – it is only in stories that people do that and Scheherazade was a purveyor of stories. She *was* the story, indeed; the symmetries and resolutions of fiction were not for her. Nor for the Sultan, poor fellow. Poor fellow? With his record? Ah, but he was a reformed character. Tamed by narrative. The sting drawn; the fires banked. He had revised his opinion of women. He loved his wife. He took a benign interest in his children. He hadn't beheaded anyone in years. He was running to fat and looked rather less like Omar Sharif than he had done in his heyday. He drank a lot of coffee and watched videos and paid desultory attention to the family oil business. Sometimes he accompanied his sisters and his old mother to London or to Paris for the shopping season. Life wasn't bad, not bad at all. A little on the quiet side, maybe – once in a while he would feel a twinge of guilty nostalgia for the old days – but agreeable enough. And he was married to the most beautiful and talented woman in the eastern world, was he not?

There was just one problem.

Scheherazade, you will recall, was an accomplished young woman even before her fateful encounter with the Sultan. She had degrees in philosophy, medicine, history and fine arts, to which she had now added doctorates in comparative literature and philology. She taught creative writing, she ran crèches and family-planning clinics, she advised governments on women's issues. At forty-two she was as lovely as ever, if not more so, and being a devoted wife she never allowed her commitments to keep her for long away from the Sultan. A night or two occasionally, no more. Their marriage, after all, had its own tradition, its internal structure, its story that could not be interrupted.

For Scheherazade had continued to narrate. After the first thousand nights there had come the second thousand, and the third, and the fourth. Where they were now the Sultan had no idea; he knew only that he was advancing towards old age with Scheherazade's soft and compelling voice still narrating to him across the pillow, night after night after night. There was sometimes an admonitory edge to the mesmeric flow, and he was certainly not allowed to fall asleep; he would jerk himself back to consciousness to find Scheherazade's incomparable eyes staring stonily at him over the embossed satin sheets from Harrods, while her elegant finger tapped irritably at the sleeve of his pyjamas. 'I'm sorry, my dear,' he would say. 'I must have dropped off for a moment. No reflection on you. Marvellous stuff, as ever. Enthralling. It's just that . . .'

'It's just that what?' inquired Scheherazade, icily.

'It's just that I get a bit lost sometimes,' apologized the Sultan. 'You're using some rather confusing words these days, you know. What does sensibility mean? And I get muddled about the settings. Where's Devonshire?'

Scheherazade gave him a freezing look. 'When you've stopped yawning,' she said, 'I'll continue.'

The trouble was that the stories had got longer and longer and, in the Sultan's opinion, a great deal less gripping. The backgrounds had become more and more exotic and the pace, in his view, slower and slower. The characters bewildered him: all these Elizas and Janes and Catherines. They talked and talked and nothing much happened except that occasionally there was a restrained social event or someone got married. He wondered, secretly, if Scheherazade was losing her touch. The trouble did not lie with him, he felt sure; he'd always been a man for a good yarn. After all, what was it about her that had bewitched him in the first place? Apart, of course, from her physical charms, which were as they had ever been – he had no complaints in that quarter. Except that . . . well, the spirit was willing but the flesh perhaps not quite as game as it had been in its prime.

The Sultan sighed and composed himself to listen. 'It is a truth universally acknowledged,' intoned Scheherazade 'that a single man in possession of a good fortune, must be in want of a wife. And stop *yawning*!' she snapped.

Time passed. The narratives continued. The Sultan was

far too much in awe of his wife to complain again. He disliked domestic dissension (this may seen startling, given his past, but remember that we are dealing with a remarkable instance of personality change). And in any case, he did not want the stories to stop, he just wanted to get back to the old days.

He was brooding upon all this one afternoon when Dinarzade paid him a call. Dinarzade, you remember, was Scheherazade's younger sister and indeed had played a crucial role in the events of the wedding night. Latterly, though, the sisters had grown apart somewhat. Dinarzade, who was studying sociology at university, had fallen in with a fundamentalist sect.

Dinarzade settled herself on a heap of cushions at the Sultan's elbow and began to chatter about a party she'd been to, tucking into a box of Turkish delight as she did so. She was almost as lovely as her sister, but very differently turned out. Dinarzade was dressed according to her beliefs (or according to something, at any rate). She wore the chador, and was veiled; her dark and lustrous eyes were all that the Sultan could see of her face. Her body, too, was covered. The general effect, though, was not one of propriety, female reticence and religious piety. Her ankle-length garment was made of cyclamen satin; her pretty feet peeped out from beneath it, shod in high-heeled shrimp-pink silk slippers. Her veil sparkled with sequins and silver beads. She wore pale lilac lace gloves. Quite a lot of her bosom was visible between veil and neckline. The bosom, in Islamic lore, is not a sexually provocative area: it is hair and hands that inflame. The Sultan had always found women's bosoms quite as alluring as any other part and hence had never known whether it was he who was perverted or traditional wisdom that was faulty.

He averted his eyes from the luscious contour of Dinarzade's breasts and sighed. The sigh had in fact nothing to do with frustrated lust but everything to do with the Sultan's more pressing preoccupation.

'What's the matter?' said Dinarzade. 'You're looking down in the mouth.'

'I am feeling a bit low,' confessed the Sultan.

'You poor old thing,' cooed Dinarzade. 'I know what you need – a good cuddle . . .' She moved closer to the Sultan.

'It's very nice of you, my dear,' said the Sultan, with a further sigh. 'But believe it or not I'm even losing heart in that area these days.'

'Can't get it up?' inquired Dinarzade sympathetically.

The Sultan winced. Not for himself but for his sister-in-law. He was old-fashioned where women are concerned (well, we know his track record, don't we?) and he didn't like to hear language like that from a nice girl.

'That's not quite the problem,' he said with dignity. 'It's a spiritual malaise, rather. To be frank, it's the stories. Your sister . . . well, to my mind she's gone right over the top. She's getting more and more experimental. We haven't had a djinn or an ogre or a youngest son or a poor fisherman in years. I never know what's coming next. And they're so long. And the characters are so dull. All these girls agonizing about their state of mind.'

'No love interest?'

'There's usually a love interest,' the Sultan admitted. 'But it's all so far-fetched you can't make head nor tail of it. We had one that went on for weeks about people shouting at each other in some place called Yorkshire where they have the most appalling weather. And then no sooner were we through with that than we were off on one about an extraordinarily tiresome young woman who marries a fellow much older than herself and then gives him the run-around. I'm pretty well at the end of my tether. I'll be a nervous wreck before the year's out.'

'Shame . . .' said Dinarzade, taking a bite of Turkish delight. 'She used to be able to do ever such a nice romance.'

'Oh, romance . . .' said the Sultan scornfully. 'It's not the romance I miss. What we never have these days is action. I want some action. Adventure. Feats of daring. Heroism and endurance. Crime. Sex. Violence.'

'I tell you what,' said Dinarzade, 'why don't you have a go yourself?'

The Sultan turned to stare at her with blank amazement. 'Me? *Me?* What an extraordinary idea! I couldn't do that sort of thing! I mean – that's women's stuff. One isn't . . . well, one is differently equipped. Tell stories!' He laughed lightly.

'Oh, well,' said Dinarzade. 'If you're not capable of it . . .'

The Sultan bridled. 'I imagine that one would be *capable* of it. It just hasn't occurred to one to try.'

It was at this point that Scheherazade walked into the room. The Sultan hastily picked up the newspaper and began to study the oil prices. His wife glanced disapprovingly at her sister and said, 'What's that ridiculous outfit supposed to mean, Dinarzade?' Dinarzade twitched a pink satin slipper and glimmered over the top of her veil.

Scheherazade wore a cream wool Armani suit with a skirt short enough to make the most of her exquisite legs. Her black hair lay in shining waves upon her shoulders. She sat down, kicked off her Kurt Geiger shoes, fished her glasses out of her bag and put them on. She had taken to wearing very large spectacles with light tortoiseshell frames although she was not, so far as the Sultan knew, short-sighted. They were extremely becoming but also intimidating. The Sultan was intimidated right now; he whipped out a calculator and frowned sternly at the oil prices. 'Had a good day, dear?' he inquired.

'Interesting,' said Scheherazade. 'And ultimately productive, I think. I am working on the initial stages of an ambitious scheme for setting up creative writing classes in the Sahara. Very exciting, but there are some initial difficulties with literacy that we have to overcome. What have you been doing?'

'Working,' said the Sultan vigorously.

He had, of course, dismissed Dinarzade's absurd suggestion. Indeed, had it come from anyone else he would have felt his manhood to be impugned and would have taken appropriate steps. But Dinarzade . . . the silly girl had always been allowed a certain licence, one could let it pass.

And then matters came to a head. That night Scheherazade began a new story. 'Tonight,' she said 'we are starting something rather special. It is a narrative which deals with the interior life of a woman. She is not a typical woman but we may perhaps think of her as a quintessential woman, or indeed human being. Her name is Mrs Dalloway. You may at first find the ambience and the presentation a little alien, so you will need to pay particular attention. And please . . . you have developed a bad habit of fidgeting. Don't. This style of fiction is extremely cerebral and I need to concentrate in order to do it justice. Are you ready?'

After three nights the Sultan's spirit was broken. He could stand no more, he realized. He had to do something. And it was then that Dinarzade's proposal came back into his head. Well, he thought, I wonder . . . Maybe . . .

All that day he paced the palace gardens, alone. His brow was creased in concentration; his eyes were glazed. From time to time his lips moved. Occasionally he flung himself upon the grass and stared up into the sky. And when the night came he laid his proposal before his wife. With dignity and with firmness.

Scheherazade was thunderstruck. Silenced, indeed. For the first time that he could remember the Sultan saw her at a total loss for words. Then, eventually, she began to laugh.

'Your turn! Well, by all means, if that's what you want . . .

But ... forgive me ...' – for a moment she was quite overcome with hilarity – '... I mean, it is *too* absurd ... But of course – you must. Please go right ahead.' And Scheherazade propped her head on her elbow and looked across at the Sultan, tolerant and amused.

Two hours later the Sultan ended his tale. He glanced warily at his wife.

Scheherazade stifled a tiny yawn. 'Not bad. It had its moments, I suppose, if you like that kind of thing. Quite good narrative drive. Rather crude characterization. Far too much rushing about on horseback and waving swords.'

'That was the point,' the Sultan protested. 'It's a war story.'

'Quite,' said Scheherazade. 'Never mind.' And she gave him a kindly little kiss on the cheek, turned over and went to sleep.

The Sultan persisted. Indeed, it was not really persistence that was needed, he found – now that he had got started he was quite carried away. There was more to this than one had thought – it could become quite obsessive. He never knew himself what was coming next. There were so many different ways of doing it. He spoke with tongues, night after night.

'... A Colt Army .45 looked like a toy pistol in his hand. "Don't nobody try to fancy pants," he said cosily. "Freeze the mitts on the bar."'

Scheherazade gave a little groan. The Sultan broke off. 'What's the matter?'

'*Another* of those ... There's a certain stylistic panache, I grant you – but what's the point of it?'

'Someone's going to get killed . . .' explained the Sultan.

'Yes dear, I realize that.'

'. . . and then you have to find out who did it and why.'

'Who cares?' inquired Scheherazade.

The Sultan ignored her. He listened, lovingly, to his own voice: 'The Indian threw me sideways and got a body scissors on me as I fell. He had me in a barrel. His hands went to my neck . . .'

He experimented. He roamed wider and further.

'What's a ray gun?' said Scheherazade with a sigh. 'And why are they going on about this galaxy?'

'They're in a spaceship. Please don't interrupt.'

'Forgive me. But again, one asks oneself – what is it all *about* ?'

'It's allegorical,' said the Sultan with sudden inspiration. He smirked. Scheherazade, thrown, glared at him across the pillow. 'Zap! Vroom! Pow! Gotcha!' continued the Sultan. Scheherazade closed her eyes wearily.

He had taken on a new lease of life. He was filled with a sense of purpose; he felt younger and more vigorous. He thanked heaven that he had realized his potential in time – there would be no more frittering away of his talents on pointless matters of business and finance. Any fool could do that. He went on a diet, had his moustaches trimmed and waxed, discarded his suits and took to wearing flowing robes which, he felt, expressed his artistic temperament rather better.

'How's it going?' asked Dinarzade. 'I love the dressing-gown thing, by the way. Really sexy. Very Clark Gable.' She patted the silken folds of the Sultan's garment.

The Sultan twirled a moustache. 'I think one might say without undue immodesty that it's going rather well. One is into one's stride. One has grasped the essentials.'

'And *whose* idea was it?' purred Dinarzade.

But the Sultan was far beyond giving credit where credit was due. 'The key to it all,' he told Dinarzade, 'is action. Get the action right and the rest follows. You know – shooting things and bullfighting and catching enormous fish and getting drunk and behaving with amazing nonchalance when fatally wounded. I've got some terrific ideas. Marvellous stuff. Can't fail.'

'Sounds great,' said Dinarzade. 'Is there any love?'

'Of course. Doomed love, naturally. To be honest, it brings the tears to my eyes.'

'How does *she* like it?'

'Your sister,' said the Sultan peevishly, 'has a one-track mind. I produce the most stunning piece, a real cliff-hanger, and all she does is go on about content and relationships. It's *got* content, I tell her – things are happening, aren't they? And my characters have very interesting relationships – they kill each other and rescue each other from hideous fates and make passionate love. What they don't do is sit around endlessly talking.'

Nevertheless, he was more affected by Scheherazade's strictures then he cared to admit. All right, so she wanted content, did she? Relationships. She wanted depth. Very well, then.

The Sultan flung himself into it. He abandoned himself to his Muse and let fiction flow. He narrated like a man possessed. He unfolded teeming sagas of poverty and social injustice swarming with vibrant characters, lurid with the din and stink of nineteenth-century London. She wanted characterization, didn't she? Atmosphere? He grew tired of that and summoned up tales of passion, power and betrayal in fields and cow byres. Inflamed with his own fluency, he was barely aware of his audience. Once or twice, pausing for breath, he noticed Scheherazade, listening now with a rather different look in her eye. 'Good stuff, eh?' said the Sultan.

Scheherazade sniffed. 'I wouldn't try that one about the man auctioning his wife outside these four walls, if I were you. You'd get ripped apart by the critics.'

The Sultan switched tactics yet again. He plunged into the dark reaches of the human spirit; his men and women seethed and fought and expounded.

'Sex in the head?' said Scheherazade. 'That's a new one on me.'

'Me too,' agreed the Sultan. 'But it's intriguing, don't you think?' He took to the sea in ships; he roamed to the far corners of the earth; he told of love and war and crime and retribution. It was as though he were driven by some irresistible force, and when from time to time he glanced at his wife he saw on her face the pleading look that he knew had once been on his own. But he could not stop; there was no mercy for either of them; he was all set to go on for ever. And then, one dawn, the children came bursting into the room and clustered around the end of the bed. The Sultan broke off. The children clamoured for attention and one of them cried, as children will, 'Tell us a story!'

The Sultan looked at Scheherazade. A strange gleam had come into her eye. 'Very well,' she said. 'Sit down quietly and I'll begin.'

The children sat. The Sultan made himself more comfortable upon the pillows.

'Once upon a time,' said Scheherazade 'there was a poor fisherman . . .'

The First Wife

At his niece's wedding Clive Harper fell in love with his first wife. At least that was what it felt like. There she was, not seen for many a long year, and he found himself in a turmoil. He stood staring at her through the chattering groups. Mary. Older, greyer, but unaccountably alluring. He was startled by his own response. Women of his own age did not appeal to him, generally speaking. His present wife was ten years younger.

It had not occurred to him that Mary might be at the wedding. He now remembered that she had always kept up with his brother and sister-in-law, with whom he himself was not on particularly close terms. He was looked upon with slight disapproval, which amused him. Well – they would, wouldn't they? He contrasted with satisfaction his own vigorous and varied life and their staid and complacent routine. Moreover, his brother was always taken for the eldest, though he was in fact four years younger than Clive. Gratifying, that.

Clive surveyed the room. A dull gathering, on the whole. Neighbours, old friends, the statutory sprinkling of relatives.

Gaggles of young – the niece's cronies. There was only one person here he wanted to talk to.

He watched her being patiently nice to an ancient aunt of his. Mary had always been good about that sort of thing. He edged nearer, to inspect more closely. She hadn't seen him yet. She of course would be expecting him to be here, so there was not for her the element of surprise. She presumably anticipated a meeting. And the very fact that she was here must mean that she . . . wanted to see him? He felt a further thrill of interest.

She was looking handsome – distinctly handsome. She seemed somehow more positive than the Mary he remembered. There she stood, a tall woman in a light green suit, with greying hair becomingly arranged, a creamy silk scarf knotted at her neck. Good legs, elegant shoes. Clive noticed this sort of thing about a woman. Mary had not used to dress thus, in the old days. He observed the pretty Victorian brooch on the lapel of her jacket and her unusual silver earrings. No rings on her hands. A warm, responsive smile on her face as she talked to this importunate aunt.

He was overcome with a quite desperate sense of loss. There she stood, who once had been entirely his, and who no longer was. She seemed a reinstatement of his own past, of his own unattainable youth. A miraculous reincarnation – tangible and present. All he knew was that he had to be near her, had to talk to her, had to have her turn that smile upon him.

He quite forgot that he had left her, all those years ago,

because he was suddenly aware that she had begun to look old. Someone had said jokingly that she looked like his mother. A young mother, mind, the person had added hastily – but the damage was done. Clive had gone home in a state of jitters, and a month later he had left Mary and moved in with Michèle, who was twenty-four and half French, an irresistible combination.

He was terrified of age. The terror had begun – oh, back in his twenties when he had looked around and realized with surprise and dismay that there were others younger than himself. His thirtieth birthday had risen up and smashed into him like a rock in a tranquil sea. He was incredulous. Thirty? Me? And then he had rallied and told himself that thirty was nothing, thirty was fine. Well – no great disaster, anyway. But he found himself looking in the mirror more often, and watching the faces of his contemporaries to see how he was doing by comparison. And every now and then there would come one of those moments of chilling realization. Thirty-six. Thirty-nine – Christ! Forty.

He was forty-one when he left Mary. She had never understood his fits of terror. She had made light of his panic, when she perceived what he felt. Look, she had said, so what? You're getting older. So am I, so's everyone. She simply didn't understand. She had no conception of those awful seizures – the cold fear in the stomach. No, no – this can't be happening. Not to me. To other people, maybe. Not to me.

And now he was fifty-nine. Sometimes, in dark moments,

the awful fact reared up and sent him reeling. But he had learned, over the years, how to keep it all at bay. Activity was the thing. Fill the days, the evenings. Travel. Go out. Be with others. Talk, laugh. He made sure to surround himself with younger people. When his old friends showed signs of becoming a touch decrepit he slid away from them. And of course Susan, his present wife, was not yet fifty.

The arrangement with Michèle had not lasted long. Indeed, he could barely remember Michèle now. She had had many successors, over the years. Little affairs – never intense enough to rock his marriage (one must have a base, a calm centre), just something to keep the adrenalin flowing. He had to have that constant frisson of interest – the anticipation of a discreet meeting, the flattery of a new face turned attentively to his.

And now – astonishingly, bewilderingly – here was Mary's face with all the allure of some stranger sighted and marked down. She was still talking to the aunt, still had not seen him. He thought with a pleasurable tingle of how she might respond when she did. How would he look to her? He was glad he had put on his rather dashing new shirt. Susan had pulled a face, for some inexplicable reason – had got out a plain white one and proposed that instead. Thank God, though, that Susan had woken with what looked like incipient flu and had decided to cry off the wedding. What luck.

He would have expected that by now Mary would be

wondering if he was here, would be casting furtive glances round the room. She did not. She continued with her patient attention to the aunt until some acquaintance joined them, when she took the opportunity to slide gracefully away. But still she did not search for him. She walked over to his brother and sister-in-law and stood talking and laughing with them in a casual intimacy that had Clive in a sudden fret of jealousy.

He tried to remember what news of her had reached him over the last few years. She had never remarried. There had been a relationship that had lasted for some while but he knew that it was over now. She was alone, he was sure of that – if she were not he would have heard. She lived alone and worked in hospital administration, a career on which she had embarked after their marriage broke up.

Long ago now, all of that. He could no longer remember very precisely the sequence of events. Just that catastrophic remark by some acquaintance, and his jitters. Michele hoving upon the scene with her beguiling youth. The way in which he himself had flailed between guilt and the panic-stricken knowledge that he was going to do what he subsequently did. He had to – it had been inevitable. And there had been outrage. His brother and sister-in-law had not spoken to him for a year. One or two friends had dropped him. And of course Mary had been badly hurt. He could see that now, could feel compunction. He had behaved badly – he would be the first to accept that.

And now was his chance – not to make amends but to

initiate a new, rewarding relationship. This was so very much what he needed, he suddenly realized. Not some transitory flirtation with an agreeable newcomer, but a dependable, mutually supportive liaison with the person he had once known best in the world. It need not affect his marriage in any way. The thing would be tactfully concealed, and provide a marvellous private uplift for them both. He was amazed still at the excitement the sight of her had induced in him.

His brother and sister-in-law had been distracted by other guests. Mary was alone. It was time to act. She was already moving away.

He arrived at her side. 'Well! . . . It's wonderful to see you, Mary.'

At the sound of his voice she turned her head. There was no surprise on her face – indeed no identifiable expression at all. 'Hello, Clive.'

'Well!' he said again. He put everything into the look he gave her. He was good at that kind of tacit eloquence, he knew. His look conveyed admiration and regret and pleading anticipation. It told her that he admired her appearance, that he thought she seemed years younger than he knew her to be, that he had a thousand things to say to her, that he needed time in which to say them. It told her, in effect, that he had fallen in love with her. Clive had himself been on the receiving end of such looks in his day and knew them to be instantly unsettling. He waited for Mary to display unsettlement.

She did indeed seem taken aback. She was silent for a

moment, apparently studying him. Then she said, 'I gather poor Susan's got flu.'

This was not the direction in which he meant them to go. He dealt quickly with Susan's flu and tried to bring things back to a more personal focus. He asked where she was living, and was told. Good – now he could get her address and phone number from the directory. He inquired about her work, and was given a dispassionate account of what she did. She was quite high-powered, he recognized. This also was disorienting, like her dress and manner. The earlier Mary – his Mary – had been a more self-effacing person. But this authority was undoubtedly part of her new appeal. A woman of her time, he thought approvingly. Good for you. He finished what he was saying – something about his own present doings – and gazed at her again with unashamed admiration. Let her know what he was feeling, what he was thinking.

She seemed a touch restive. She glanced over his shoulder, sipped at her drink. She was affected by him, no doubt about that. He had disconcerted her. Now, perhaps, was the moment to make a direct approach.

'Could we perhaps . . . meet?' he said.

She hesitated. And now that wretched aunt was heading for them.

'Mary,' she was crying. 'Mary – I quite forgot to give you my new address.'

Clive gave his first wife his most beseeching smile. 'Soon? I'll call you. All right?'

She seemed about to speak, hesitated again. And then the aunt was there, chuntering on. Clive touched Mary's arm for a second and left them.

He could understand her hesitation – he could sympathize entirely. She didn't know how to respond. She mistrusted her own feelings, perhaps – was confused by the whole encounter. He would wait a couple of days, and then phone her. No – he would write a brief note first, maybe send some flowers, phone the day after that.

For the rest of the afternoon he made perfunctory conversation with others while trying to keep Mary within his sights. He did not manage to speak to her alone again, and when he searched for her to say goodbye she had already gone. Never mind, the groundwork had been done.

He decided against the flowers – a banal touch, that would be. He wrote her a letter – short but intense. He told her how deeply moved he had been at seeing her. He hinted delicately at years of regret. He implied a sense of void in his own life. He included one or two veiled references and muted jokes which referred back to their life together. He concluded by saying that he wanted very much to see her. Perhaps they could meet for lunch or dinner? He would phone her next week.

She did not reply. He had anticipated this – naturally, she would not wish to seem precipitate. He called, and was confronted with an answerphone. He rang off without leaving a message, and tried again the next evening. Still the answerphone. This time he spoke. He proposed lunch in three days' time. He named a restaurant. If he did not hear from her he would take it that this was acceptable and would look forward with immense pleasure to seeing her.

He arrived slightly late at the restaurant, stymied by traffic. Handing his coat to the waiter, he looked round anxiously – no sight of her. Good – it would not do to have kept her waiting. And then the waiter said, 'A lady came earlier, sir. She left you this note.'

Clive stared at the man. He took the envelope. He felt a trickle of fear. He sat down, pulled out a single sheet of paper, and began to read.

Dear Clive: No, thank you. Not lunch nor anything else. I wonder what makes you think I should wish to? Well – empathy was never your strong point.

Your letter implied a certain desolation – nicely understated but poignant none the less, which was no doubt the intention. A state of mind with which I have been deeply familiar. However, I am not I feel the right person to offer solace. I'm sure you will find someone more receptive, unless you have entirely lost your touch, which everything suggests that you have not.

Thank you for your compliments – most acceptable to a woman of my age. You haven't changed all that much yourself, though more I fear than you would like. The signs of a desperate rearguard action are plainly visible. You seem anxious to remind me of the old days, so I'm sure you won't mind if I presume on former intimacy and make a point or two. The hair *en brosse* is not a good idea, and I wouldn't tint the grey bits if I were you – it shows in a strong light. Also, the puce shirt is unwise on a man of your age and figure. I do hope Susan's flu is better. Poor thing. Yours, Mary.

'Would you care for an aperitif, sir?' the waiter was saying.

The Butterfly and the Tin of Paint

This is a story about a tin of paint and a prime minister. It seems also to be an eerie reflection of the butterfly effect. The butterfly effect illustrates chaos theory – that intriguing explanation of physical events which proposes that a very small perturbation can make things happen differently from the way they would have happened if the small disturbance had not been there. Thus, a butterfly in the Amazon forest flaps its wings and provokes a tornado in Texas. Other variations have the butterfly in Adelaide and the storm in Sussex, but the implications are the same and we don't need to know what kind of butterfly it was either.

The irritating thing about the butterfly effect as a theory is that you are never given an account of the progression from the wing flap to the tornado. The butterfly moves a wing and generates presumably a current of air. Then what? This is where scientists do not always deliver the goods. Real life, on one hand, and fiction, on the other, leave nothing unexplained. There is a reason for everything, in life as in art. Whether this story is life or art or neither is for the reader to decide. One thing is certain: it is not science.

The tin of paint was a trade size drum of Dulux Gloss White. It had been acquired by a decorator called Pete who was painting and wallpapering the bedroom of some people called Ambrose who lived in Fulham. The Ambroses do not come into this story. They are an absence, though a significant one, because if they had not elected to have their bedroom redecorated none of these events would have taken place. They were absent – on holiday in the Algarve – when Pete began work on their bedroom one Tuesday morning and even more mercifully absent when, at 8.35, he stumbled and kicked over the open tin of Dulux Gloss White.

The paint gushed in a viscous flood all over the Ambroses' bedroom carpet, which Pete had not covered with plastic sheeting as an efficient decorator should. He stared in horror and then rushed around the house looking for cloths. After another fifteen minutes he realized that more drastic remedial measures were called for. He leapt into his van and drove off in search of a hardware store that could supply carpet cleaning materials. He was in a total panic, because his wife had just had a baby and he desperately needed the money from this job. When eventually he located a promising-looking shop and drew up outside it on a yellow line his panic made him do something he had never done before. He left the van unlocked and tore into the shop, his head full of queries about carpet cleaning techniques.

Pete's negligence was noted by a seventeen-year-old opportunist called Lennie who was standing outside the shop drinking a tin of Coke for breakfast, with nothing in particular in mind for the foreseeable future. Lennie knew exactly what to do under these circumstances. He whipped open the bonnet of the van, started the engine and was into the driving seat and off while Pete was still discussing paint removers with the assistant in the hardware shop. Lennie's plan was to nip straight to the estate where he knew some of his friends would be hanging out, also with no specific plans for the day, go through the contents of the van to see what was resaleable and then all have a bit of a joyride down the M4.

He had been driving for only three or four minutes when he heard the banshee wail of a police car. Lennie's response to a police siren was instinctive – he simply slammed his foot on the accelerator. As it happened, the police car was about quite other business and knew nothing of Lennie or the van. Lennie hurtled round a corner, lost control of the steering and the van skidded into the back of a builders' lorry which was temporarily parked outside a café while the driver got himself a cup of tea.

Lennie did the sensible and expedient thing. He abandoned the van and disappeared. By the time the lorry driver came roaring out of the café there was a driverless white van with broken windscreen and crumpled bonnet embedded in the tailgate of his lorry.

The van was immobilized and had to be prized away by a breakdown truck. The only serious damage to the lorry was a burst back tyre. The lorry driver set about changing the tyre, seething with rage. He was already well behind schedule and would catch merry hell from his employer, who was on site awaiting delivery of the load of planks in the back of the lorry. After half an hour the van had been removed and the tyre changed. The driver bounced back into his cab and revved off at some speed. In his haste to get going he had not noticed one further piece of damage. The impact of the van had snapped one of the tailgate locks and loosened the other, so that it was no longer securely fastened.

The lorry driver, anxious to make up for lost time, hurtled through south London with the load of timber jouncing furiously behind him and slamming into the insecure tailgate each time he accelerated. The surviving lock eventually sprang apart in a one-way street down which he sped in search of a short cut. The planks broke free and shot out into the road. Three taxis which were also taking advantage of what was in fact a well-known rat run piled up behind the spilled planks and the stationary lorry and were at once neatly trapped by a brewer's truck which turned off the main road just in time to plug the street completely. The lorry driver climbed down from his cab and began wearily to retrieve the planks while the taxi-drivers sat in their throbbing vehicles and listened to Capital Radio.

The street was still blocked when an apprentice taxi-driver who was on a moped doing the knowledge tried to edge past the brewer's truck. He was practising the run from Gray's Inn Road to the Elephant and Castle, which should by rights take him along here. Seeing that this route was out of the question just now he swerved back into the main road in search of an alternative way and swung round a corner into the next side road, rather too fast, at the same moment as the Filipino houseboy of a foreign diplomat stepped off the pavement.

The Filipino houseboy was exercising the diplomat's two young Rhodesian ridgebacks. The dogs were on leashes but even so not sufficiently under control. One of them shot out of the gutter as the moped turned the corner, utterly disconcerting the apprentice taxi-driver, who mounted the kerb and ended up in a tangle on the pavement with the Filipino, who let go of the leashes in the confusion.

The Rhodesian ridgebacks were delighted. It is not a lot of fun being hauled around the streets on the end of a leash when you are nine months old and bred to a peak of perfection. They shot off like bats from hell, careered the length of several streets and fetched up in a garden square where they roamed around for a while until they spotted a cat furtively crossing the road. They homed in on it at thirty miles an hour.

The cat raced up the trunk of a chestnut tree and sat quivering in a fork fifteen feet above the dogs, who ran up and down excitedly for a bit and then got bored and wandered off, thus dropping out of the story, as do the apprentice taxi-driver and the Filipino houseboy. Actually, the Rhodesian ridgebacks turned up soon after in Brompton Road, where they caused a major traffic incident and thus triggered several other chaos sequences with which we cannot be concerned. The apprentice taxi-driver and the Filipino struck up an acquaintance which developed in a rather interesting way, but we cannot be deflected by that either, I'm afraid.

The cat was a young Burmese which belonged to the ten-year-old daughter of a divorced fashion designer who lived in the square. The child looked out of the window and spotted her darling mewing pathetically from the fork of the chestnut tree in the square gardens. Mother and daughter rushed out with a tin of sardines and a broomstick.

Fifteen minutes later the two of them were still standing at the foot of the tree, fruitlessly calling the cat and proffering sardines on the broomhead. The kitten wept and clung to the tree. The fashion designer, who had a client due shortly, began to get restive. The daughter became hysterical. At this point their next-door neighbour, a rather well-known theatre director, came out of his house intending to pick up some milk from the corner shop. Seeing this imbroglio, and being a decent fellow, he volunteered to fetch his extending ladder and retrieve the cat. The offer was accepted with gratitude.

The theatre director climbed the ladder and grabbed the cat, which promptly bit him, thus making him lose his balance. He slipped, slid awkwardly to the ground and broke his ankle. The cat was fine.

The director was due shortly at a rehearsal of the play he was currently directing. From the Outpatients Department of Charing Cross Hospital he used his mobile phone to notify all concerned that the rehearsal would have to be called off. The leading lady made noises of false regret and moderately genuine sympathy. In fact she could not have been better pleased. She had just embarked on an amorous involvement with a famous playwright, of whom she was not seeing enough owing to pressure of work commitments. As soon as the director was off the line she called her lover to announce that – surprise, surprise – she had a free day ahead. The playwright was delighted and proposed lunch at their favourite restaurant. The actress set about making herself look even more delectable than she did already and in due course was seated in a discreet corner of the restaurant gazing into the eyes of the playwright.

Their presence was noted by a journalist who made a point of visiting that particular restaurant at regular intervals to see who was consorting with whom. He worked for a tabloid newspaper and was even more devoid of moral scruples than others of his kind – a majestic example of the breed, shall we say. He watched the playwright holding hands with a lady not his wife, identified her with interest, and when they left he decided to follow them. The trail led him to the entrance to an apartment block in a side street not far away, where the couple vanished, presumably into the actress's apartment for an afternoon of dalliance.

The journalist called up his paper and told them to send along a photographer. He had better things to do himself than hang around any longer, but one of the boys could stake the place out and maybe get a nice pic to go with tomorrow's story if and when the pair emerged.

Thus it was that a bored photographer was huddled on the step of the apartment block entrance at six o'clock that evening, wearing a grubby sweater and holding out an empty tin, with his camera discreetly stowed behind him, pretending to be a street beggar. He did not at first recognize the prime minister when the latter ran swiftly up the steps and pressed the Entryphone bell to one of the apartments. The photographer simply shook his tin and chanted, 'Spare any small change?' Then he looked at the prime minister again and did a double take.

The prime minister ignored him. He was used to such figures and indeed had uttered many public pieties about the problem of youthful vagrancy. In any case he had other things to think of right now. It is not easy for a prime minister to carry on a sexual liaison. They are busy men, apart from anything else. But where there is a will there is a way, and the prime minister had perfected a system of clandestine visits to the object of his attentions which had worked efficiently for many months now. The lady in question was the former wife of a political associate, an attractive enough woman but not one to set the world on fire and many would be surprised that he saw her as worth the risk. But there is no accounting for passion, as we all know. Suffice it that it is probably true to say that our man was the first prime minister since Lloyd George to conduct an undetected adulterous relationship.

The prime minister had left his car discreetly parked around the corner, and his security guard with it. The story was that he was paying a duty call on an elderly relative. Whether or not the chauffeur and the guard fell for this routine is not known. Necessarily each visit was brief, given the prime minister's schedule – an hour or so, at the best of times.

He rang the bell. The photographer listened intently. He heard the prime minister's voice – quite distinct and familiar – saying simply, 'It's me.' And then he heard another voice, unmistakably female, somewhat amplified by the Entryphone: 'Hello, darling.'

The photographer rose to his feet, faint with excitement. He saw the prime minister vanish into the apartment block. The photographer stood there for a few moments, quivering like some sleek carnivore that has scented prey, and then he began to plan the days ahead, which might stretch into weeks. He would need time, patience and equipment. The hidden mike, the concealed camera. Well, we know the arrangements, don't we?

In the event he struck gold within a fortnight. The prime minister resigned a few days later. The nation's press carried on the front page similar photographs of his expressionless face, seen in profile through the window of the car which bore him to the Palace.

Pete, the decorator, saw it on the front of his copy of the *Sun* as he went to work in the Tube, but he did not pay it much attention. Prime ministers come and go, and in any case he had problems of his own. The insurance company had not yet paid out on the van, the Ambroses were back and their bedroom carpet was a write-off.

Crumbs of Wisdom

'I've never heard of Ruth Harrap,' said Clive Morland.

Elaine, the tutor, laughed. 'Of course you have, Clive. All those lovely romantic historical novels one read when one was fifteen. Not up-market literary stuff, I know, but real craftsmanship. We can all learn from a writer like that.'

'I read animal books when I was fifteen.'

The members of the Creative Writing Group were a disparate lot, united only in their resentment of the tutor. Elaine was a published writer, and her two novels, long out of print, could occasionally be tracked down in public libraries. The only member of the group who had achieved print was Clive, a retired teacher, who had two articles in professional journals and a piece in the *Guardian*, some years ago. There was a tacit acknowledgement, though, that papers and magazines did not really count. It was only a real book that signified. There was a splinter movement among the younger members of the group, who had their sights on television and fought a relentless battle for more discussion of drama and situation comedy writing. The age range ran from the three sixth-formers to a group of over-sixties who had long since abandoned any desire or intention to publish and specialized in destructive criticism of anything that anyone else wrote.

'I don't see why we can't try Martin Amis,' said Lucy, one of the sixth-formers.

It had been Elaine's proposal that they should vary their usual routine of fortnightly discussion meetings with an annual visit to an author.

Sylvia, one of the over-sixties, a founder member of the group who long pre-dated Elaine herself and hence was accustomed to pull rank, had pointed out that traditionally the group always made its annual outing to a famous literary house. 'We're due for Chawton again this year.'

But Elaine, in the event, had won the day. The argument switched to which writer should be visited. Interest mounted, names were bandied around. Fay Weldon? Anita Brookner? Len Deighton? Controversy raged, with literary affiliations pitilessly exposed. The group became polarized between those lobbying for names of popular acclaim and those sternly determined on established quality. Jeffrey Archer was set against Iris Murdoch. The young proposed figures unheard of by the rest of the group. Clive Morland suggested J. B. Priestley; when it was pointed out that Priestley was no longer alive he retired into a sulk from which he emerged only to rubbish other nominations.

They reached tentative decisions. Elaine was deputed to ring up the publishers of a popular crime writer, and reported that they had not been at all helpful. She wrote to a well-known woman novelist, and received no reply. It was at this point that she began to press for Ruth Harrap.

'I've heard of her,' said Sylvia. 'I've read her. She's like Barbara Cartland, only less so, if you see what I mean. You used to see hundreds of her on station bookstalls.'

'She'll be dead, I don't doubt,' said Clive.

Elaine smiled sweetly. 'As a matter of fact she isn't, Clive. She's getting on, but that's no crime, is it? Actually she wrote me a rather nice letter once, years ago, after I'd written to tell her what pleasure her books gave me when I was a girl.'

The group eyed her, stonily.

'Actually I suppose you could say that in a way she was a sort of influence. When I started writing seriously myself my early work owed quite a bit to her style. Of course I was doing something rather more complex – more ambitious, I suppose you might say, and when *Tigers of the Night* came out I can see that not many readers would have seen any connection but . . .'

'Pity there wasn't,' said Sylvia. 'Or you'd have been selling in hundreds on station bookstalls.'

The teenagers giggled. Elaine, with difficulty, maintained her smile. 'If indeed one had been aiming at that sort of market.'

'I want to go and see the Barbara Cartland lady,' said Lucy, 'if we can't have Martin Amis. She'll wear pink ostrich feathers and diamond rings like knuckledusters. And there'll be blue satin sofas and pomeranians. It'll be hilarious.'

And so it was decided. A few weeks later Elaine announced with satisfaction that she had a reply from Ruth Harrap. 'She'd love us to come. Isn't that marvellous! Tea, she says. At about four.'

'That's a let-down,' said Lucy. 'I thought we'd get pink champagne.'

Elaine ignored this. 'Her house is called Foxdene. I think that's after one of the books. *Foxdene* was the eighteenth-century one, I'm sure, with the consumptive heroine and the mad poet. Aren't we lucky! She remembers me, I imagine – I sent her a copy of *Tigers of the Night*, actually, when it was first published. One of the things you must all remember, if and when you publish, is the importance of complimentary copies. Bread upon the waters, you know.'

'Let's see her letter,' said Sylvia. A forthright retired librarian, her principal activity as a member of the group nowadays was to query Elaine's leadership and refer obliquely to the superior skills and status of previous tutors. The group regarded this running warfare as good spectator sport: the honours were usually about even.

Elaine handed over a single sheet of paper, with a touch of reluctance. Sylvia studied it.

'She doesn't say she'd love us to come. She says bring your group to see me if you wish. She doesn't say anything about remembering you.'

'The letter was presumably dictated to her secretary,' returned Elaine. 'One doesn't go on at great length in an official letter.'

'If that's the case she needs a new secretary. There's two mistakes there. And the typewriter's out of the ark.'

Elaine sighed. 'We don't all of us share your passion for technology, Sylvia. It's not what you write *with* that matters, as I'm for ever saying, it's what you write. And I think we're very privileged to be making this visit. Now, let's get on, shall we? We've all been reading Keith's story and we're going to discuss. Clive, would you like to start?'

'I counted five sentences ending with a preposition. He can't spell pyjamas or marmalade. A short story should be three thousand five hundred words long and by my reckoning this is all of five thou. He's got this bloke driving from London to Cheltenham on the M4 and I can tell you for a fact . . .'

The group braced itself for action.

On the day appointed for the visit to Ruth Harrap they assembled at Elaine's house. Despite the steadily falling rain there was a festive atmosphere and an exceptional camaraderie. Outfits appeared that had never been seen before. A couple of the older women wore hats: several of the men had put on suits. The sixth-formers were tidier and more scrubbed than usual. Elaine herself was resplendent in lilac with a general effect of trailing chiffon and tinkling costume jewellery. She was in a state of exhilaration in which bossiness combined with slightly manic arguments about the route and who should go in which car.

'Now listen, everybody, do remember that this isn't just a fun occasion, there is a serious purpose as well. We're going to have the chance to talk to a very celebrated, very successful author, even if she's not as well known just now as she once was, and it's the most marvellous opportunity to pick up a few tips. Crumbs of wisdom. So do . . .'

'If we don't get moving soon we're not even going to get crumbs of chocolate cake,' said Clive. 'Come on. Marching orders.'

'All right, all right. Now I think if I go with Keith, in front, plus Lucy and the other girls, and if Sylvia . . .'

Arguing, clutching hats and umbrellas, the group piled into the cars.

Two hours later the leading car came to a halt. The others drew up behind. Everyone got out and gathered around Elaine, who seemed perturbed. They were on the outskirts of an undistinguished small town, beside a petrol station. Traffic flashed along a bypass.

'Lost, are we?' said Sylvia with satisfaction. 'Wouldn't you know it!'

'We're not lost,' said Keith, a normally unshakeable VAT inspector who appeared at this moment to be on the brink of some kind of outburst. He had, of course, just experienced two hours of Elaine. 'We're not bloody lost at all. This is what the directions said, to a T. That's got to be the house.'

He pointed. The group stared doubtfully at the building next to the petrol station, a large, dour, box-like bungalow guarded by a rigid square of conifers. There was a pervading smell of petrol and the relentless shush-shush of traffic. Rain fell. A cedarwood sign beside the front gate said 'Foxdene'.

'So here we are!' cried Elaine, pulling herself together. 'All present? Right, then!'

She marched up the concrete path to the front door, with the group straggling behind, and rang the bell.

There was a pause. The group dripped. 'I'd imagined something rather different,' said Sylvia. 'Regency mansion, that sort of thing. Or a nice Georgian rectory, even.' Elaine glared.

The door was opened, at last, by an elderly woman in a shapeless tweed skirt and grubby sweater. Elaine smiled uncertainly: 'Miss Harrap is expecting us.'

'Come in.'

The group shed coats and umbrellas in a dark hallway smelling of yesterday's dinner. They were ushered into a sitting-room where those who could sat, and the rest perched on the arms of sofas. Their guide inspected them for a moment and then dumped herself down in the desk chair. It occurred to everyone that this was, in fact, Ruth Harrap.

The group dealt with the situation in various ways. The sixth-formers nudged each other and tried to stifle their reactions. There was an outbreak of that sudden searching for handkerchiefs and fervent inspection of surroundings that indicates collective embarrassment. Elaine launched into a hectic account of their drive. '. . . but as it turned out Keith was absolutely right. I *had* muddled up the two roads, so we doubled back and here we are! I can't tell you how thrilled we feel, Miss Harrap! But let me introduce everyone . . .'

Ruth Harrap listened impassively. When Elaine was

through she spoke at last: 'If anyone wants the doings it's along the passage and turn left.'

The group rustled and cleared throats. 'Not right now, thank you so much,' said Sylvia.

'What we're longing for is to pick your brains a bit,' said Elaine. 'May we? Can I start? For instance, do you like to write in the morning, or are you a night person?'

Ruth Harrap considered. She had straggly white hair of the kind that has yellowed in places, and wore a hearing-aid. At last she said, 'I don't like to write. Never did. Gave it up years ago, thank God.'

Elaine smiled indulgently. 'Oh, of course we realize you're not doing as much as you used to. But writers never really retire, do they? I mean, I'm mostly tutoring these days myself but one is always first and foremost a practitioner, even if one's output slows up.'

'Elaine wrote a book called *Tigers of the Night*,' offered Lucy. Innocently, or so it seemed.

'Haven't heard of it,' said Ruth Harrap.

'Bread upon the waters . . .' murmured Sylvia, *sotto voce* but not quite *sotto* enough.

Ruth Harrap rose and left the room, without explanation.

'Do you think she's gone to get tea?' said Elaine wildly. 'Maybe we should offer to help. Lucy, why don't you . . .'

There was a disturbance among the occupants of the sofa. A dog, in appearance like a decaying bath-mat, and evidently of great antiquity, had emerged from beneath and was making a tour of people's legs, snuffling.

'Pomeranians,' said Lucy. 'Blue satin.' The sixth-formers collapsed into giggles.

'Oh, for goodness sake . . .' snapped Elaine.

At this moment there came the unmistakable sound of a lavatory being flushed. Ruth Harrap re-entered the room, adjusting her skirt, and sat down again without a word. The group fidgeted uneasily.

'Have a look round the garden if you like,' said Ruth Harrap.

The group gazed out of the window, beyond which the conifers and a rectangle of lank grass were almost obscured by a curtain of drizzle.

'Well . . .' murmured Elaine. 'What we're all wondering,' she went on brightly, 'is . . . what advice would you give to the aspiring writer?'

'The who?'

'Aspiring writer. The . . . you know . . . person who wants to write.'

'You needn't spell it out,' said Ruth Harrap tartly, displaying her first sign of animation. 'I couldn't hear you, that's all.' She paused. 'Don't. That's what I'd say.'

Elaine laughed merrily. 'Oh, I do understand. I mean, in my humble way I've toiled in the vineyard as well. I *know*. It's gruelling, Punishing. But the rewards, Miss Harrap! And I don't *of course* mean financial rewards. The artistic satisfaction. All that.'

There was a silence. The author stared at Elaine, her face knotted in disapproval. 'That may be your experience, for what it's worth. It's not mine. I never wrote but for cash. I wanted to be a buyer in a department store. Never got promotion. Ten years in china and gifts, I was, and then all those books, and I don't know which was worst.' She heaved herself to her feet again. 'You'd better have some tea before you go. How many with sugar?'

'Lucy, perhaps you girls could go and help Miss Harrap,' said Elaine, in a strangled voice.

The group sat in silence. From the kitchen came the clatter of crockery, and, surprisingly, sounds of merriment. Elaine sat studying a picture above the mantelpiece, wearing a pinched expression. The others took turns rebuffing the dog. Their hostess and the three sixth-formers returned, bearing a tray with mugs of tea and plates of Jaffa Cakes and Tea-time Fancies. 'Pass the plates round, dear, will you,' said Ruth Harrap to Lucy. It was clear that some kind of accord had been established.

They drank, and ate. Their hostess had a conversation with the girls about the dog's ancestry: she demonstrated how he could sit up and beg for a biscuit. Sylvia made an inquiry about the name of a plant on the window-sill, which prompted a desultory horticultural exchange. Cups and plates were gathered up and returned to the trays.

Elaine rose. She had recovered her composure. 'We really mustn't trespass on your time any longer, Miss Harrap. This has been so kind. I know we're all tremendously thrilled – it's an experience we shall treasure.' She smiled graciously.

Ruth Harrap surveyed her visitors. She appeared to be

making some kind of assessment. 'That's forty pounds,' she said. 'Three pounds a head and half price for schoolchildren. I'll knock off the odd fifty pence.'

There was a stunned silence. 'I'm sorry?' faltered Elaine.

'You wanted to come and see me. I didn't particularly want to see you. It seems to me fair enough.'

Elaine gaped. Then she forced a laugh. 'Of course. I take the point entirely.' She delved in her bag. 'I haven't actually got . . . Will a cheque be all right?'

'A cheque will do,' said Ruth Harrap.

They collected their coats and umbrellas. They filed out on to the pavement again. Elaine brought up the rear, her head held high, her face wearing once more the pinched expression. Everyone avoided her eye.

'Poor old soul,' said Sylvia.

Clive snorted. 'Poor old soul nothing. Sensible lady, and good luck to her.'

'She can't ever have been the type for ostrich feathers anyway,' said Lucy. 'Actually she was rather nice.'

Elaine rallied, with an effort. 'What you all have to remember is that art and eccentricity often go hand in hand. Artists are unpredictable people. Writers come in all shapes and sizes.' She began to perk up, warming to her theme. 'And of course a true professional, like our good hostess, is not going to reveal the mysteries of her craft just like that, is she? There's a certain sense of privacy. Not to mention the difficulty of actually communicating the essence of . . .'

The other members of the group were already sorting

themselves out into the cars. 'Come on, Elaine,' said some-one, briskly.

No one talked very much, on the return journey. The sixth-formers were especially quiet, busy planning for themselves careers in merchant banking, computer programming or the fashion industry.

Loved Ones:
A Christmas Fairy Tale

It is indeed a fine thing to be amid one's loved ones at the festive season. Yes, said Sylvia Cramp to her neighbour Sydney Tyler (going on seventy, both of them – on their own but making the best of it) – yes, the girls are all coming, and their boyfriends (no one gets married these days, do they?), they like a proper Christmas and the way they live, with their jobs and that, how could they find the time to set it up? And yes, said Sydney, I'll be going to mine, as usual. I'll have a couple of days with the one – they want me to do a spot of decorating for them while I'm there, they don't have a moment themselves, of course. And then I'll pop over to the other – promised I'd mind the kids for a night or two, give her a break, fair's fair. Ah yes, they agreed, it's a time you want your family around you, isn't it? So, said Sylvia, I'd better be on my way, get stuck into the shopping, seven we'll be, and the girls like things done nicely – choosy, they are, my girls. 'Bye then, Sydney.

Smoked salmon, they had said, and fruit and nuts of course, and Stilton and Bath Olivers and liqueur chocs and so forth, and be sure and get good stuff, Mum, won't you?

No junk. Money's not a problem – we'll settle up with you later. Money we have – it's time we're short of and anyway you love doing Christmas, don't you? Goose, not turkey – turkey's out these days. Oh, and not a pud – pud's out too – make something frightfully elaborate and amazing of your own, we'll leave it to you, you're such a super cook.

One of the girls bought leather coats for a famous department store, the second owned a chain of florists, the youngest ran an employment agency. They all earned thousands and thousands of pounds every year, had enormous mortgages, sheaves of credit cards, high blood pressure, therapists and naturally they couldn't cook. They ate in restaurants or not at all. They doted on their mother and they sometimes still brought their washing home for her to do and *of course* they always came to her for a lovely traditional Christmas with all the trimmings, bringing with them their boyfriends, who had migraines, high blood pressure, hundreds of credit cards and permanent jet lag.

Don't bother with the drink, darling, they said – we'll have it sent, you might go wrong there, it's not really your thing, is it? Just see to the food. Oh, and remember lots of Perrier, and croissants for breakfast, and do one of your incredible home-made soups for Christmas Eve lunch and we must have crackers and chestnuts and a six-foot tree.

Sylvia Cramp went to the supermarket. Once, twice, thrice. Festooned with shopping-bags, peering at lists, she fought her way from Fresh Meat to Dairy to Household Goods;

she stood doggedly in checkout lines; she toiled like a dray-horse up the hill back home. Several times she met her neighbour, Sydney Tyler (a really nice fellow, Sydney, when you got to know him – missing his wife, of course, poor man). When she got back to the house, like as not the phone would be ringing as the girls remembered further essential items: marrons glacés and After Eights and you will make a cake Mum won't you? One of them had seen this fantastic recipe for crab mousse – nice for a starter, you'll have fun with that, Mum. Another had forgotten to mention that the new boyfriend was a vegetarian – just do him something simple, a quiche or a lasagne. They telephoned from offices and from restaurants and from parties and from airports – breathless and busy: they hadn't got a moment, they said, can you lay in orange juice and muesli and yoghurts and wholemeal bread? We're exhausted, they said, we're just going to come to you and *collapse*. Oh, and can you be a darling and do us a Caesar salad for Boxing Day, and there will be dates and grapes and a prune stuffing for the goose, won't there?

Sylvia trudged to the shops and back again. And again and again. The fridge was filled and the freezer and cupboards and shelves. She cleaned the house and made up the beds and several times she took a break and had a chat with Sydney – nice Sydney next door. The girls rang to say that their blood pressure was up and they thought they would exchange this lot of boyfriends for another lot and that they were simply longing for Christmas. Have fun, Mum, they said. But don't overdo it — we just want a simple family Christmas.

On Christmas Eve Sylvia prepared the kitchen. She took the goose from the freezer and put it on the windowsill. She set upon the table potatoes and sprouts and onions and oranges and lemons and eggs and gelatine and sugar and very much else besides. She went upstairs and when she came down she was carrying a suitcase in one hand and a letter in the other. The letter she placed upon the kitchen table. It said: 'To make soup, chop vegetables for many hours. For cake – mix, whip, etc., until exhausted. Ingredients for crab mousse and Caesar salad and prune stuffing and elaborate dessert in fridge.' Sylvia went into the hall, where were several boxes delivered by the Wine Society; from these she extracted a bottle of Moët et Chandon champagne and another of Château La Tour-Carnet. After further thought, she added to these a bottle of Glenfiddich. She then put on her coat, gathered up the suitcase and the carrier bag with the Wine Society bottles, and went down the garden path to the taxi in which Sydney Tyler awaited her, with a fond smile upon his face and two air tickets to Tenerife in his hand.